Kopi Luwa[illegible]:

World's Most Expensive coffee beans from civet poop Or An Urban Myth?

Facts and information on history, where it is grown, habitat of civet - its daily care, breeding, premium coffee imitation, cost, places to buy, coffee making process and how to store

Copyright and Trademarks

Disclaimer

IBS Publishing Limited takes no responsibility for, and will not be liable for, the websites being temporarily unavailable or being removed from the internet. The accuracy and completeness of information provided herein and opinions stated herein are not guaranteed or warranted to produce any particular results, and the advice and strategies, contained herein may not be suitable for every individual.

While every attempt has been made to verify the information shared in this publication, neither the author nor the affiliates assume any responsibility for errors, omissions or contrary interpretation of the subject matter herein. Any perceived slights to any specific person(s) or organization(s) are purely unintentional.

We have no control over the nature, content and availability of the web sites listed in this book. The inclusion of any web site links does not necessarily imply a recommendation or endorse the views expressed within them.

The author shall not be liable for any loss incurred as a consequence of the use and application, directly or indirectly, of any information presented in this work. This publication is designed to provide information in regards to the subject matter covered.

The author has taken utmost care to confirm the accuracy of the content; however, all readers are encouraged to follow information at their own risk. The author cannot be held responsible for any personal or commercial damage that results from misinterpretation of information, negligence or otherwise.

What Will You Find in this Book

As some of us are aware of, Kopi Luwak or civet coffee is the rarest and most expensive coffee available today. People have been reviewing, discussing and talking about this unique coffee because of its exclusive harvesting process and unique origin.

For coffee lovers around the world, this is a must have item, despite its high cost. Most coffee connoisseurs do not mind spending on coffee that is of such exceptional quality.

This book is written to guide you and give you information about this rare and very unique type of coffee that is in demand by coffee lovers from different corners of the world. In addition to the history and harvesting process of this unique coffee, I have also shared details about the Indonesian native animal, Civet that is the main character behind the entire Kopi Luwak story.

The Kopi Luwak coffee has also been in news due to the controversy around the way the civet breeding is done and the issues around animal care in such commercial domains. I am totally in support of the fact that the organizations involved in producing Kopi Luwak coffee should be following the appropriate guidelines, laws and treat these beautiful creatures with respect & care.

Read through the book and learn everything you want about Kopi Luwak, including the best places to find the most authentic coffee in different regions of the world to help you enjoy the best and most precious coffee in the world.

For more information, please go to the following site:
http://www.kopiluwakcoffeefacts.com/

Keep reading and enjoy!

Acknowledgement

I was very fascinated by the topic of Kopi Luwak and fondly remember its mentioning in the movie 'Bucket List' (2008) where the character played by Morgan Freeman reveals the true fact behind the source of Kopi Luwak coffee to his friend played by Jack Nicholson. To quote the exact words of Jack Nicholson in surprise - 'You are shitting me', to which Morgan Freeman had replied – 'No, the cats beat me to it'!!

This was a fascinating topic for me to pursue and to provide as much relevant information as possible to the real coffee enthusiasts, to satiate their demand on more information and facts about this truly amazing coffee of this world.

Thanks to my family and friends for their support and belief in me to get this book out to my readers. Hope you will enjoy it.

Table of Contents

Chapter 1: Introduction – Is Kopi Luwak Real or an Urban Myth?

- Is Luwak coffee or Kopi Luwak an urban myth?
- Is the consumption of Kopi Luwak safe for human beings?
- Are there any chemical changes and taste changes in the beans of Kopi Luwak coffee during the process?
- Is Kopi Luwak the only food consumed by humans which is first digested by an animal?

Keep reading to get your answers:

The word coffee refers to the Spanish word, Coffeea. It is one of the most consumable drinks after water, and is liked by a majority of people in the world. Other than that, it is also the second largest commodity traded in the world, after oil.

To date, many people are unaware what Kopi Luwak is all about. Surprisingly, some of the local Indonesians haven't heard this name before. This type of coffee is so unique and unusual that many people believe it is a myth. A number of people argue that Kopi Luwak is either a legend or a complete myth; however, this statement is now denied.

There is no doubt about the existence of Kopi Luwak; at least not after Oprah Winfrey tried the rarest and most expensive Kopi Luwak coffee on her show.

To clarify more on this topic, a food expert, Dr. Massimo Marcone from the University of Guelph, Ontario, Canada, was given a sample of this coffee. He was asked to analyze Kopi Luwak to find out if there is any difference between ordinary coffee and this rare Kopi Luwak. At first, he was shocked to hear about the existence of such a coffee, but later the proposal was accepted.

The results showed nothing particular or unique about the coffee, except for its process. However, with more observations carried out, Dr. Marcone noticed under a scanning-electron microscope that the beans of Kopi Luwak coffee possess surface micro-pitting. This was only visible at 10,000 times magnification.

This is not present in ordinary coffee beans. The food expert believed that this difference was the result of the enzymes present in the civet's stomach, which influenced those proteins within the coffee beans.

Many other revelations were made which will be discussed later in the book. For now, to keep up with your curiosity about Kopi Luwak, the unique coffee is known for strong and rich aroma, while the taste is fully bodied and incredible.

The texture of the coffee, once prepared, is syrupy and thick with a mesmerizing hint of a chocolaty and clean, long aftertaste that will linger on your tongue.

Heard about Jacu Bird Coffee? To your surprise, Kopi Luwak isn't the only consumable food item for human beings that is first consumed by an animal. In Brazil, a bird known as Jacu eats ripe coffee berries and just like Luwak, and defecates in the jungle. The local Brazilians collect these to get the Jacu Bird coffee out of it.
Is that too much information? Craving to know more, already? Let's start with the detailed history of how Kopi Luwak came into being.

The Discovery of Kopi Luwak

With the varied range of different types and quality of coffee available, people fond of this aromatic drink had been in the run to get their hands on the finest quality of coffee available in the market. Kopi Luwak, also popularly known as Civet coffee, is native to Indonesia, has set unquestionable standards in beverages, making it irresistible to try this unique coffee at least once in their lifetime. It is one of the most expensive coffees in the world at the moment due to its unique flavor, taste and aroma.

As far as the history of coffee is concerned, it goes all the way back to around 800 B.C. It was discovered by Kaldi, a shepherd in Abyssinia (now known as Ethiopia). One day, the shepherd found out that his goats couldn't sleep for the whole night after eating some kind of berries. These were coffee-berries. To satisfy his curiosity, Kaldi also tried those berries and suddenly felt a flow of a different, pleasant feeling within his body.

After a few years, the discovery of Kaldi travelled all the way to Arabia, where Arabian people discovered a more advanced method of coffee-berries. This was popularly known as 'Qahwa'. The meaning of this word is strength or power because the plant's extract were of extremely high energy.

Various other countries adapted the name, which went through various changes to become what we call today as coffee. Coffee beans were exported from Arab to other countries. However, only coffee beans that were fully processed and ready-to-be-served were exported. Thus, there was no way for it to be cultivated in the rest of the countries.

After the 16th century, Baba Budan, an Indian pilgrim, managed to take coffee beans out of Arab for the purpose of plantation. During the year 1615, coffee made its way to Europe, through the Venezia traders. By the year 1616, Dutchmen were the people to cultivate coffee plants in Europe for the first time. Later, Dutchmen took the coffee plant to their colonial countries for cultivating it, which also included Indonesia.

The Arabica coffee plant was introduced in Indonesia for the first time during 1696 via Sri Lanka. The establishment of the cash crop plantation was initiated by the Dutchmen in West Java, which later spread to the provinces of Sulawesi and Sumatera.

According to the resources, Indonesia was the country that discovered Kopi Luwak for the first time. This discovery was made during the era of political cash crop plantations carried out by the colonial Dutch government in Indonesia. And then came the day when plantation workers discovered coffee beans covered in the Luwak droppings in the forest.

The coffee beans were taken home, where the workers cleaned and roasted them. They prepared and drank the coffee made from those beans. The unique flavors and taste was surprising to the workers, which definitely was more delicious and much better than regular

Eventually, there was more coffee to meet the demand of the people. Unfortunately, due to extremely high prices (with additional cost associated with extra labor force), people started backing off. Some people couldn't afford the high prices altogether while others believed the price was not worth the product.

There seemed no way to balance the demand and supply of this unique coffee. However, experts found a way to tame wild civets. This is what farm civets are all about. Farms were established and civets were kept in a domestic environment and were fed fresh coffee berries to produce droppings that could provide maximum coffee beans possible.

While the initial fixed cost of setting up farms was high, the variable cost decreased instantly. Since the civets were not in the wild anymore, the droppings were easy to collect within the cage or the secluded area the civets were kept in.

This enabled the suppliers to control their day to day costs, which had a positive impact over the prices of Kopi Luwak. As soon as the prices were set back to previous prices, the demand rose again. People who couldn't afford Kopi Luwak because of its extremely high prices were able to invest in the world's most unique coffee once again while people who thought Kopi Luwak wasn't worth the price didn't mind giving it a chance out of curiosity.

Finally, the demand and supply set an equilibrium price on the graph. However, as more time passed, Kopi Luwak kind of disappeared. There was no hype about the coffee and people were not talking about it.

It wasn't until Oprah Winfrey tried Kopi Luwak on her show and referred the coffee from the Sumatra Islands of Indonesia to be the world's best coffee, that people realized its existence. People who considered Kopi Luwak as a myth also came to know the reality of this coffee and showed interest in trying it out.

Once again, the demand for this coffee was increasing, and suppliers around the world were eager to serve the demand. Kopi Luwak, like other unusual and rare items, faced fluctuations in both demand and supply throughout this time. However, because of its unique process and incredible attributes, it is still the world's most expensive coffee.

I spoke about Farm Luwak above. Farm Luwak and Wild Luwak, what is it all about? You will learn more about this in detail later in this book.

Different Types, Different Flavors

Other than rarity, taste is the most important factor why Kopi Luwak is highly demanded and highly prized. The distinctive properties of Kopi Luwak make it one of the most desirable beverages available today. As far as the taste is concerned, there are no types or flavors available for Kopi Luwak.

However, some objective assessments of taste are present. Kopi Luwak, as you all know, are coffee beans collected from the waste products of Asian civets that are cat-like animals. Hence, there can be variation in taste due to the origin and type of beans consumed, processing following collection, ageing, roasting and brewing.

In addition, the ability of the animal to select the right berries as well as aspects associated with the health and diet of a civet (e.g. the quality of berries provided or stress level due to an unhealthy habitat) can be some of the most prominent influencing factors that can affect the processing as well as the taste.

This is where the quality comes in. When people pay a huge amount to get a single cup of coffee (sometimes in the range of GBP 60 or USD 100), they definitely want the best and finest quality coffee available. It is highly recommended that you only buy from authentic suppliers or sellers in your area. Of course, there are many people who sell regular coffee as civet coffee to make more money. Do not get fall for that, especially if you are buying civet coffee online. The best way is to do a little research and check for authentic customer reviews. You can even ask a family member or friend who have tried Kopi Luwak and knows an authentic seller or supplier.

An entire chapter has been covered with these important details. Refer to them in the end to get the best quality coffee with the most distinctive and strong taste to have a lifetime coffee drinking experience.

Green Beans – Are They Kopi Luwak Too?

Just like other coffee, green is the actual color of Kopi Luwak beans. The color isn't clearly visible until the beans are through the cleaning and drying process. When the civets excrete the coffee beans out, the color at that time is also green. However, it can't be clearly seen because of the poop around it.

The coffee is in different shades of green until it is roasted. Most people pay for the final product, i.e. the roasted coffee. However, there is also demand for green unroasted coffee beans. You can find some with authentic dealers out there. You can roast them according to your personal preferences and use them accordingly.

So if you see green Kopi Luwak beans somewhere, don't simply think of them as fake. They could be real Kopi Luwak, just unroasted. Besides the quality of coffee beans, roasting is a very important factor that determines the taste, color and aroma of coffee. It wouldn't taste perfect if it's underdone or overdone.

The beans should be roasted to perfection, available in the suitable aroma, color and taste for your consuming pleasure. Regarded as rich, amazingly flavored, strongly full-bodied, Kopi Luwak is distinguished because of its exceptional syrupy and chocolaty hint in taste. Even after you have consumed the coffee, you can still savor the lingering, clean aftertaste.

The flavors are complex, and Kopi Luwak is the perfect combination of all the pleasurable flavors you can find in all the best coffees – musty, earthy, heavy-bodied, syrupy sweet and aromatic. The acidity level is low in Kopi Luwak while the flavor profile is as exotic like no other. In short, the authentic flavor of Kopi Luwak coffee is indescribable even to coffee connoisseurs.

Is It Safe?

The experience of novelty of drinking this exotic and rare coffee cannot deny the fact that this coffee was excreted by a civet. For most people, hearing about such processes can be nauseating. When most people hear of anything like that, they distort their face in disgust. This is one of the main reasons why most people think that drinking Kopi Luwak may not be safe for humans.

However, there is a scientific research available to prove these people wrong. A study conducted at the University of Guelph in Ontario, Canada, revealed that the extensive process of cleaning and the insignificant availability of bacteria in Kopi Luwak make it a safe coffee to drink. The research has showed that the coffee doesn't present any danger of presence of E.Coli (rod-shaped bacteria commonly found in the lower intestine of warm-blooded organisms) in this coffee.

Watch this video for more information:
http://www.youtube.com/watch?v=Dv0Gtc-lhzw&feature=youtu.be

The brewing and roasting process eliminates all bacteria due to the high level of heat. So if you had any doubts whether you will get sick after consuming Kopi Luwak, remember that the digestive process this coffee goes through is only done in order to modify the coffee beans.

If you are sensitive to caffeine altogether, or have any condition in which you are not sure whether or not you should consume any type of coffee, avoid Kopi Luwak. Otherwise, it's all good to go.

Chapter 2: The Role of Civet in Kopi Luwak Preparation Method

In the process of obtaining Luwak Coffee or Kopi Luwak, there are two main participants: the human and of course, the animal.

The civet plays an important role in giving us the most scarce and best coffee. It is the civet (also called Paradoxurus Hermaphroditus) that eats the coffee berries and as a result, excretes the coffee beans out, which then goes under a long process to become drinkable.

This chapter will focus on the process of Kopi Luwak, the origins and processing as well as Farm Luwak and Wild Luwak.

The Exclusive Way to Get this Coffee

Kopi Luwak is a gourmet coffee prepared from the finest quality and ripest coffee berries that are first eaten by an animal. As mentioned earlier, the cat-like animal, civets, local to Indonesia, eat the coffee berries and pass it through their digestive systems. The berries are digested but the beans present inside them pass undigested through their system.

The civet then graciously deposits the dropping on the floor of wild jungles and forests, where local coffee farmers are eagerly waiting to collect it. This natural process of getting the Luwak Coffee or Kopi Luwak only takes place in Indonesia, usually near the islands of Sumatra, Bali, Sulawesi and Java.

It is the civet that selects the ripest coffee berry plants and eats the entire fruit. However, the little animal is unable to digest the seed (which is actually the coffee bean) and excretes it out among its faeces.

Chapter 2: The Role of Civet in Kopi Luwak Preparation Method

This is the simplest way to put it:
Civet + Coffee Berries = Kopi Luwak

The established businesses in Indonesia have hired local farmers to collect the faeces from the forests and jungles of Indonesia, and this is where the human part starts.

The most natural way to get the best Kopi Luwak coffee is described in detail below. This method is still used in Indonesia. Most of the process requires labor and the coffee roaster is usually the only machine that is being used in the process of obtaining the real Kopi Luwak coffee.

Chapter 2: The Role of Civet in Kopi Luwak Preparation Method

Cleaning:

After the Luwak faeces is collected from the forests, the farmers' cooperatives separate the layers by crumbling it. The faeces cover most of the green coffee beans. The faeces are completely separated from the coffee beans in the cleaning process.

Selecting:

The next step is to select the best beans you have extracted from the faeces. The Kopi Luwak beans are separated one by one in this process. The bad ones are kept aside, extracting the best and finest quality beans out. In addition to coffee beans, the faeces also contain other objects such as stones. Also, there are small or bad beans and all of this should be separated from the good ones.

Through this process, they are able to get the premium quality Kopi Luwak green beans that are cleaned and selected and ready to be taken to the next step.

Washing:

The Kopi Luwak green beans are washed thoroughly to remove the faeces particles and dirt. Once washed, they are immediately dried with air. If not dried immediately, they might ferment due to humidity when stored. Next, the washed and dried beans are stored in a dry, dark place until they are considered ready to be roasted.

Roasting:

It is time to roast the green civet coffee beans. Roasting coffee beans, (whether Kopi Luwak or any other regular coffee) is the most critical and important step in the entire coffee production. Roasting has significant implications on the color, aroma and taste of the coffee. Therefore, roasting can impact the overall coffee quality, giving the zest to it.

Chapter 2: The Role of Civet in Kopi Luwak Preparation Method

The body, the aroma and the taste are acquired with the bean roasting process. This is why it's said that brands achieve various types of coffee although they use the same coffee beans. There are multiple ways to roast coffee. You can simply use a pan and heat the coffee over it or get it roasted in the gas rotary drum roaster or you can even use a hot air roaster.

Most experts suggest that the best way to roast coffee beans in the best possible way is to roast them in a hot air roaster. This is because the beans do not come in contact with any hot metal part, which can roast some beans more than the rest. The control process of this roaster is electronic, which is an advantage over other roasting processes. Set up all roasting steps electronically and achieve the same uniform result every time you roast coffee beans.

As far as a general gas rotary roaster is concerned, you cannot roast small quantities of coffee beans using it. It is more suitable for commercial purposes where they need to roast a lot of coffee beans at a time. However, some home models of gas rotary are available now that can do the job for you.

If you have unroasted Kopi Luwak beans and are planning to get a gas rotary for roasting it, make sure you get the home model that can easily roast small quantities at a time. Due to the outrageous pricing, the product generally does not undergo massive production or consumption. Thus, a roaster that perfectly roasts small quantities of coffee beans will be just right for you.

People demand unroasted Kopi Luwak beans because they think that freshly roasted coffee tastes and smells much better. Roast the beans when you wish to prepare the coffee and enjoy the alluring delicacy of Kopi Luwak.

Let's get back to the roasting process. As far as the temperature is concerned, make sure it does not exceed 230°C (400°F). During the roasting process, Kopi Luwak releases sugar and oil. Also, it loses humidity and grows in size. The final weight drops down by 20 percent.

During the roasting process, the chemical components of a coffee bean go through various important transformations at both quality and quantity level. Protein, sugar, non-protein nitrogenous substances, fat, acids, etc.; in fact each and every component present undergoes a transformation due to the high level of heat they are exposed to.

Just like other types of coffees, over-roasting Kopi Luwak coffee beans can destroy its unique taste and complex flavors. To get the best from the roasting experience of Kopi Luwak coffee beans, make sure they are medium roasted and remain rich in color. Once the beans are roasted into the perfect color, they should be cooled down quickly to immediately stop the process of roasting. It will not only fix the aroma but will also condense the oil.

Allow the roasted coffee beans to rest in shape for at least 12 hours before you grind them to prepare the perfect hot cup of coffee. Once all these steps are complete, you will have the perfect ground Kopi Luwak coffee to enjoy.

Packaging:

Generally, single origin gourmet coffees, such as Kopi Luwak, are packed in the form of whole beans instead of ground because it keeps the aroma and flavor intact for longer. However, it is easy to find ground Kopi Luwak coffee if you want to avoid the whole grinding process. In such a case, a ready-to-make coffee will be available that can be prepared instantly.

On the other hand, if you are ordering whole beans of coffee, it is important that you explain your preferred brewing method to learn about the right degree of grinding suitable for your need.

Chapter 2: The Role of Civet in Kopi Luwak Preparation Method

Source: http://upload.wikimedia.org/wikipedia/commons/f/fa/Kopi_Luwak-01.jpg

There are special bags designed for Kopi Luwak coffee, which come with a one-way degassing valve. This valve allows the liberation of gases produced after the coffee roasting process and does not allow air to enter the bag and ruin the coffee. Don't forget, humidity along with some oxygen are the worst enemies of all types of coffee.

It is important to take care of things you have to pay a fortune to get. Kopi Luwak is one such commodity. Therefore, make sure you keep it away from water or any type of humidity, oxygen in the form of air as well as save it from direct exposure to sunlight.

The Origin and Processing of Kopi Luwak Coffee Beans

To round up this chapter, let's have a detailed look into the origins and processing of Kopi Luwak coffee beans one more time.

Before turning into coffee berries, all coffee begins as a fragrant, beautiful flower. They usually grow on hillsides and blanket it like perfumed snow. The flower then transforms into small green berries. These are not bigger than glass marble balls.

Inside each coffee berry, there are two coffee beans sitting adjacent to each other. However, until the berries are green they cannot be harvested. In a few months, when they are ripening to a bright, vivid red, they can be successfully harvested. Plus these berries can be eaten raw as well.

Coffee grows in a number of different countries around the world. Some varieties did better than others and gained special reputations based on a combination of particularly excellent flavor, unusual circumstances and rarity. Such coffees, from Tanzanian Pea-berry to Kona to Jamaican Blue Mountain, command an outrageous price as well. However, no other coffee, as mentioned earlier, comes in such scarce supply, has such a different and interesting background and such unique flavors as Kopi Luwak. And if you talk about price only, no coffee even comes close to the premium price commanded by this special commodity.

As far as the origin of Kopi Luwak is concerned, it comes from the Indonesian islands of Sulawesi, Java, Bali and Sumatra (formerly Celebes), which are a prominent part of the Indonesian Archipelago's 13677 total islands, out of which only 6000 are inhabited.

Native to these famous Indonesian islands, there is a small marsupial known as the civet or Luwak. This small tree-dwelling cat-like animal is a part of the sibet family. Long regarded as pests by the natives, they climb all the way to the top of the coffee trees just to feed on the reddest, ripest coffee berries.

Other than Jacu coffee that I mentioned in the beginning, there are other specialty food items in addition to Kopi Luwak that can be processed in a similar fashion. This story starts with Argan, which is a tree similar to the acacia that grows in Mexico and Morocco. The tree grows fruit that are similar to olives and are known for yielding argan oil. The Berbers in Morocco let their goats climb the trees to feed on this fruit. Later, the droppings of the goat are gathered and pits are removed, which they grind to extract oil that is used for massages, as well as an aphrodisiac.

Coming back to Kopi Luwak, which started off as a way to extract unique coffee without the need of climbing the tree, has now evolved into the most expensive specialty coffee in the world. Kopi Luwak is purchased in bulk by Japan, but M.P. Mountanos (800-229-1611), the first person who introduced the exotic coffee bean in the United States, imported 110lb (approximately 50 kilograms) of Kopi Luwak after spending around 7 years in search of a stable and reliable supplier in 2009.

According to Mark Mountanos, Kopi Luwak is indeed the rarest beverage in the world. He had no regrets of spending almost a fortune in getting the best quality coffee all the way to the United States.

When Richard Karno, the former owner of 'The Novel Café' based in Santa Monica, CA, received a flyer from Mark Mountanos introducing Kopi Luwak in the United States, he thought it was a joke. However, he realized that it was true and immediately ordered 1 pound (around 450 grams) of Kopi Luwak due to curiosity. Richard Karno was the first man in the United States to send releases in the local press inviting them over for giving a cup of Kopi Luwak a try. When no one responded or turned up, he got the exotic beans roasted and made some coffee for himself and his staff.

Chapter 2: The Role of Civet in Kopi Luwak Preparation Method

Richard Karno was the next person who converted to Kopi Luwak and was very enthusiastic about it. According to him, it was the best coffee he ever tasted. He highlighted the attributes of the unique coffee by calling it heavy bodied, with a caramel-like strong taste. The way he described the aroma was jungle-like green and musty, which roasted really nicely.

On the other hand, Mountanos shared his views calling it a coffee with the most complex taste and flavors, attributing the unique flavors to the natural process the exotic coffee beans undergo when they are still in the paradoxurus's (civet) digestive system.

He believed that the enzymes and acids present in the stomach are the components that give this coffee its unique aroma and taste. The coffee with the heaviest body, musty tone and earthy flavors was now on its way to popularity once again. The unique aroma and its syrupy structure were two attributes that were most talked about. There are even reports that even Starbucks bought Kopi Luwak from Mountanos.

Chapter 2: The Role of Civet in Kopi Luwak Preparation Method

Chapter 3: Learning All About a Civet

The Asian Palm Civet is known as Luwak in Indonesia. It is one of the species of small mammals that belong to South East Asia and Africa. Another generic Malay name for any fox or cat-like animal that does not specifically refer to the Indonesian Luwak is known as Musang.

Source: http://upload.wikimedia.org/wikipedia/commons/f/f7/Luwak.jpg

It is not the Kopi Luwak that brings Civets in association with humans. They have a history, where humans used the African civets as a major source of musk, the fixative base of various popular perfumes as well as the most expensive known animal product.

In addition to Indonesia, Luwaks can be found throughout tropical East Asia including Vietnam, India, Sri Lanka, Philippines and

Malaysia, where these little mammals inhabit tropical rain forests as well as coffee plantations and fruit yards.

Luwaks basically live on trees and since they are omnivorous, they can eat anything they find available. Naturally, their diet is made up of eggs, small animals, and insects and of course, the fruits in season.

When it's time for coffee plantation to harvest, Luwaks consume the coffee berries in abundance and then consequently deposit Kopi Luwak. The bright red coffee berries become the major part of the Luwaks' diet that helps us get lots of Kopi Luwak through the Luwaks' droppings. But this is not all. There is much more to learn about this unique animal and the unique Kopi Luwak that comes as a result. Read on to learn more.

The Perfect Habitat

Geographic Range

The Asian Palm civets are native to regions within and around Asia, including India, Bhutan, Bangladesh, Nepal, Thailand, Sri Lanka, Myanmar, Peninsular Malaysia, Singapore, China, Vietnam, Cambodia, Laos, Brunei Darussalam, Sarawak, Philippines, Sabah and the Indonesian Islands of Siberut, Bali, Bawean, Kalimantan, Java and Sumatra. This rare species of cat-like mammals were introduced to Japan, Sulawesi, Maluku and Irian Jaya, the Lesser Sunda Islands. However, the presence of Asian Palm Civets or Luwak is uncertain in Papua New Guinea.

Characteristics

Another very common name for Asian palm civets is 'weasel cats'. This is because the animal resembles both the weasel and the cat. The Luwak or Asian Palm Civet averages 7 pounds (3.2 kilograms) in weight, has a body length of 21 inches (53 centimetres) and a long tail of around 19 inches (48 centimetres). Its stocky, long body is layered with shaggy, coarse greyish colored hair, with black on its muzzle, ears and feet.

The Asian palm civet has an elongated body with short legs and a very long tail. The small nose protrudes from their face and is quite pointed. Their face is similar to cats but their skulls are flatter and longer. While they have a small face, they have very large pointed ears and big dark eyes. Luwaks have three long rows of black markings on their body. They usually have short hair which is grey or black in color. Over the forehead, under each eye and at the sides of the nostrils, there are white spots that add definition of color to the creature. The Luwaks are arboreal, nocturnal and solitary. Unlike other civets, Luwaks or Asian palm civets don't have black rings on the tail. Instead, they are only tipped black at the very end.

Neck hair is another distinguishing factor that draws a clear line between Asian palm civets and other civets. Asian palm civets or Luwaks grow hair backward on the neck while, the other members of the civet family have a forward hair pattern on the neck. Luwaks have more specialized teeth since they fall into the omnivorous category. Other civets have completely different sets of teeth that are designed to eat meat. In short, Asian palm civets have pointed and weaker teeth, and the carnassials, that help in slicing meat, are not completely developed.

Since Luwaks have plantigrade feet, they usually walk like raccoons or bears, with their complete sole touching the ground. Their soles are naked while they have semi-retractile claws. Their third and fourth toes are also partly fused. All these features make them amazing climbers and hunters.

Both females and males of this species have a scented perineal gland located under their tail. These glands are pretty much like testicles; the feature that earned them the scientific name, Paradoxurus hermaphroditus. There is a double-pocket pouch holding the gland under the abdominal skin. Luwaks use this gland to spray for marking territories, in defence, and to communicate with others of the same species.

Habitat

Luwaks can live in a variety of different habitats. However, they primarily inhabit local forests, but are also found at lower densities in selectively logged and secondary forests.

They also inhabit suburban gardens, fruit orchards, plantations and parks with fig trees, large mature fruit trees as well as undisturbed vegetation. They have sharp claws that allow them to climb house gutters and trees.

In various parts, especially Sri Lanka, Luwaks or Palm Civets are considered pests as they litter in attics and ceilings of common households, and create a lot of noise moving about and fighting during late night hours. The activity period, which begins from 6:00 pm till 4:00am, is subjective to daylight. Luwaks are only active once its dark and retreat to sites for resting right before dawn. Throughout the day, Luwaks sleep on high trees. These are little territorial animals. Luwaks give birth to their little ones in boulder crevices or in tree hollows. They prefer to stay in the tallest trees with vines and trees with dense canopies for protection and seclusion.

They were, however, pursued by human beings, who hunted Luwaks for damaging plantations and orchards, but since realizing the extra income they could earn for selling the faeces of Luwaks, the treatment given to them has completely changed. It seems as if Luwaks are the king of plantations in Indonesia and other areas of South East Asia, where they are found.

Behavior and Ecosystem Roles

Luwaks are actually solitary animals, meaning they spend most part of their lives alone, except during the brief mating periods. Luwaks are arboreal, meaning they live in trees, as well as terrestrial, meaning they live on the ground as well, and also show nocturnal activity patterns during late hours at night until after midnight.

Source:
http://upload.wikimedia.org/wikipedia/commons/c/ce/Asian_Palm_Civet_Over_A_Tree.jpg

Olfactory response to different excretions, such as the secretion of the faeces, urine and perineal glands as well as the scent marking behavior, greatly differs in females and males. The palm civet or Indonesian Luwak can easily distinguish sex, species and unfamiliar/familiar individuals by the smell of the secretion of perineal gland.

Availability of food and predation are the main reasons that decide the activity and social organization of Asian palm civets. As mentioned earlier, civets are actually active from dusk to dawn, while they are resting on trees during most of the day. In fact, they are said to be more active when nights are darker as compared to nights that are illuminated by the moon. They are most active as dusk starts, usually looking for food and as soon as dawn approaches, they look for a place to rest. During the sunlight hours, palm civets curl up themselves among vines, inside rock crevices and even tree holes.

Depending on the food supplies of the season, Luwaks are usually found sleeping or resting on the same trees where the supplies are steady in the region. It is also believed that the nocturnal behavior of civets actually helps them avoid active predators during the day time. Usually, Luwaks break up their activities with little 'relaxing' breaks like clawing, stretching, or grooming. As compared to female Luwaks, males are much more active while it is believed that dominant males are more active than Luwak males that are submissive.

All in all, Asian palm civets or Luwaks are more active when there are few predators and plenty of food supply. Depending on the availability and supply of food, civets also decide whether or not they should overlap territories. When there is ample food supply readily available in the region, they do not overlap the territories. However, when Luwaks are in search of food that is not available within the region, they are forced to wander into other territories in order to find food and survive.

Luwaks or Asian palm civets are both hunters and foragers. Even their behavior resembles that of cats in that they usually stalk their prey keeping themselves at a safe distance and suddenly pouncing when the prey is not prepared.

It is easier for Luwaks to jump from one tree to another in search of fruits, or dig and scavenge the ground to find worms. They are experts when it comes to climbing, aided by their grasping hind feet and claws. On the other hand, since they have a non-prehensile tail, they are considered less agile as compared to other types of civets. This is the reason they move slower than other civets and need to grasp branches to get from one tree to another.

As far as the ecosystem roles are concerned, Luwaks consume the seeds of various trees present in its region, such as that of palm trees (pinangazavana and pinangakuhlii). Primarily, they contribute to the dispersal of different seeds they consume, since the seeds pass through their digestive system and are excreted out through their faeces (just how Kopi Luwak is produced) hundreds of meters away from where the seeds were initially consumed.

In simple words, they help the forest regenerate by encouraging the seeds of different plants and trees to germinate.

Key Behavior: Solitary; Sedentary; Nocturnal; Arboreal

Average Territory Size: 17sq.km

Range Territory: 5 to 20sq.km

Ecosystem Impact: Disperses seeds

Lifespan Range: 15 to 20 years

Average Lifespan in Wild: 20 years

Lifespan Range in Farm: 15 years to 24 years & 6 months

Home Range

Generally, the home for Asian palm civets is the forested area where they spend most of their life in a typical area ranging between 1.4 and 50 sq.km. This is until they are captivated and kept in Luwak farms for producing Kopi Luwak.

A number of studies have been conducted on the movement habits and range of Asian palm civets with the help of radio tracking collars. The studies revealed that male civets have larger ranges as compared to females, at 17sq.km and 2sq.km, respectively. During the night, they travel hundreds of meters, with an average distance of 215m. This usually happens when civets are in search of food.

Communication

Typically, civets are silent animals. However, when it comes to making noise, they can be very annoying. Their sound is similar to a cat's meows. They also spit, hiss and snarl when they are harassed or alarmed.

You will rarely find these small mammals communicating vocally, except for when they are being attacked or agitated. Instead of using their vocalizations, they mainly reply via olfactory responses and use their scent glands to communicate with other members of their species. The scent glands are their primary means of communication. They can easily secrete odors for self-identification from their skin, faeces, urine and perineal glands. Also, Asian palm civets mark territories and their range by dragging their anal glands on the ground.

However, they also rub their heels and ear-neck region, and drag their anus to do the same. Again, there is a difference in how males and females practice this. Males, as compared to females, mark territories and objects more frequently using their scent. This is because male civets are more dominant and territorial than female civets.

Scents left from the perineal gland remain longer in the environment than any other scent produced by Asian palm civets. Thus, this is used as a long-term source of communication and information by this animal.

Channels of Communication: Chemical

Communication Modes: Scent marks

Channels of Perception: Chemical; Acoustic; Tactile; Visual

Predation

As mentioned earlier, palm civets possess nocturnal and arboreal characteristics. These are believed to have developed by these small mammals as mechanisms to avoid active predators. The lives of civets living in different parts of the Asian subcontinent are at risk because of larger cats, such as leopards and tigers, and reptiles, such as crocodiles and large snakes.

Known Predators:
Leopards (pantherapardus)
Tigers (pantheratigris)
Crocodiles (crocodylidae)
Snakes (reptilia)

Farm Luwak and Wild Luwak – What's The Difference?

Referring back to the history, it wasn't until late when Kopi Luwak gained all the interest from coffee enthusiasts around the world. Of course, the people living in the country, where Kopi Luwak was produced, also showed interest, not in the coffee but in the production of this unique and rare coffee to make some serious money.

Due to the unique process and low supply of Kopi Luwak, the market price of this coffee was very high and was constantly growing with time. This was attractive for businesses in the consumer market in Indonesia.

By realizing that Luwaks and coffee berries are all they need to get into the real business of Kopi Luwak, they came up with the idea of establishing Luwak farms. What initially started in a wild forest was now taking the form of a standardized farm, where Luwaks were kept, fed and bred to produce more Kopi Luwak.

Wild Luwak

Wild Luwak, which is considered a more natural form of producing Kopi Luwak, was all about collecting the Luwak droppings from the wild forests and jungles of various islands in Indonesia. The process is natural, where farmers search for as much Luwak droppings as possible on the ground.

The droppings are collected and then processed after thorough cleaning, washing and drying process. The green coffee beans extracted from the droppings of Luwaks are then either stored for roasting later or roasted immediately to prepare the world's most expensive and best tasting coffee.

There is a huge difference between Wild Luwak and Farm Luwak. The habitat and living conditions of the animals are also different. Luwaks out in the wild need no instructions. They eat whatever they find (according to the season) and excrete it out wherever they want. This makes the whole natural process difficult to collect the droppings of Kopi Luwak.

Since the production of Kopi Luwak was already in a very low quantity, searching for all the droppings in the wild forest was not an easy task. People were scared that they were losing on a lot of Kopi Luwak just because they were not able to find and process all the Luwak droppings available.

This is where the idea of Farm Luwak came into being. While the cleaning, washing, drying and roasting process remain the same, establishing farms for Luwaks to get maximum Kopi Luwak was a completely different story.

Farm Luwak

People planned to establish farms for Luwaks to make the most out of their excreted waste product that could be transformed into a fortune-making coffee. The design plan included establishing a similar habitat where Luwaks could feel at home as in the wild, as much as possible.

Instead of allowing Luwaks to choose the best and ripest coffee berries on their own, the best quality coffee berries are provided to them to consume in order to get the best quality Kopi Luwak. While Luwaks are designed to live in the wild, their farm life is maintained at the wild-life standards to give Luwaks a home-like feel while they are caged. The only purpose to put these animals behind bars is to keep them safe, in good health and gain maximum Kopi Luwak from their droppings.

Ripe coffee beans of the best quality are fed to them on a timely basis in the best possible manner. Since they are under observation at all times, keeping them in the farms ensures their good health as well. Since the Luwaks live inside the cages, it is easier to collect their faeces. All the faeces can be found within the cage which saves a lot of time and hard work.

This not only speeds up the procedure of extracting as much Kopi Luwak as possible, but eliminates the chances of missing out on faeces that has the exotic coffee beans on them. In short, this became the most effective way to produce and extract as much of these luxury coffee beans as possible.

Setting up farms for Luwaks to produce more coffee isn't a simple thing to do either. While the process of collecting faeces and extracting coffee becomes easier, the cost of setting up farms and maintaining the living standards of Luwaks is a pretty expensive and difficult job. People dealing in the supply of Luwak coffee around the world are responsible to meet the fixed and daily expenses occurring as a result.

Also, due to the recent claims by PETA, WSPA and other animal rights co-operations of keeping Luwaks in an abusive habitat, businesses owning Luwak farms now have to make sure they maintain the right standards of keeping Luwaks safe and in the best health conditions in order to keep running the farms.

Many farms even allow Luwaks to eat a combination of different foods, like they do in the wild, to get the best Luwak beans. Natural plants and trees are adjusted within the cage to give a home-like feel to Luwaks, even when they are behind bars.

As a coffee enthusiast, I also believe in fair treatment of the animals and that their habitat, living condition, food habits, health and activities be kept at a standard as if they were in the wild. The rules and conditions provided by the organizations like PETA, WSPA and others need to be followed to ensure that these lovely animals are not treated badly for commercial gain. This should be made top priority by the businesses running the Luwak farms to ensure that these animals are treated properly and the coffee enthusiasts keep getting their loved coffee with a confidence of a trusted source.

The lengthy processing period of cleaning, washing, drying and roasting coffee beans ensures that the best coffee beans are packed and exported to other countries, where coffee connoisseurs are ready to pay hundreds of dollars for just a pound of coffee.

As far as the quality is concerned, both the coffees have their own characteristics. While the coffee produced from the Wild Luwak claim better quality than Farm Luwak coffee because of the natural procedure, businesses producing coffee through Farm Luwak have their own side of the debate where they believe that a cleaner environment, better food and healthier conditions allow Luwaks to produce a better quality coffee in comparison.

People around the world crave to have a single cup of coffee, without really paying attention to whether it was produced through Farm

Luwaks or Wild Luwaks. However, on the other hand, there are people who are so particular about the authentication of this rare, most expensive coffee that they prefer to buy faeces of Luwaks with coffee beans intact, instead of the processed ones.

All in all, Farm Luwaks make it easier to extract Luwak coffee in a more effective manner, making it possible to produce more coffee beans than ever before. Unfortunately, the rise in supply had no positive effect on the price because the cost associated in the entire procedure and the high demand never let the prices come down.

It has also been claimed that with the establishment of more and more Luwak farms, the annual production of Kopi Luwak increased drastically, meeting the demands of people around the world, because more coffee was produced and in a much more efficient way.

This is because Wild Luwaks feed on coffee berries only during the coffee harvesting period. When that period is over, they switch to other feeding options such as other fruits of the season, little mammals and even insects. During this time, it becomes difficult to generate more Kopi Luwak following the natural, wild procedure.

In case of Farm Luwaks, coffee berries are provided to Luwaks throughout the year to produce more and more Kopi Luwak on a regular basis. Of course, it does not limit the people to get their hands on the best quality coffee berries, which they provide these little animals to feed on. Since Luwaks love coffee berries, they feed on their favorite meal that is provided throughout the year and produce world-class Kopi Luwak coffee beans all year long.

This is one of the main reasons why Farm Luwaks are considered one step ahead of the traditional, natural method of extracting Kopi Luwak coffee beans from Wild Luwaks.

Feeding a Civet – The Best Way to Get the Best Quality Coffee

When civets are in the wild, they eat whatever they like, including fresh fruits, vegetables and even insects. This also includes coffee berries which ultimately help them produce Kopi Luwak coffee beans through their faeces.

In principle, it is not possible to control what Wild Luwaks feed on when they are living in the forest in the tree hollows. However, by habit, the Wild Asian palm civets are known for eating the best and ripest coffee berries and other fruits available. This is one of the reasons farmers used to kill them for destroying their best fruits and plantation, until their importance in producing Kopi Luwak was discovered.

On the other hand, when kept at farms, the diet of the Farm Luwaks could be controlled by giving them the best quality coffee berries in order to provide the best possible Kopi Luwak coffee beans. On the whole, the Asian palm civet or Luwak is a nocturnal omnivore. Pulpy fruits are its primary source of food, which includes coffee berries, papaya, rambutan and mango. Luwaks are known for picking their fruit wisely, leaving fruits that are less ripe to consume at a later date.

Luwaks also prefer palm flower sap, which becomes toddy, sweet liquor, when fermented. This earned the Asian palm civet another one of its famous name 'toddy cat'. Luwaks are extremely fond of coffee berries and during the coffee harvesting time, that's the only thing they eat. Naturally, it inhabits suburban gardens, parks and wild forests with mature fig trees, fruit trees and undisturbed vegetation.

Unfortunately, many Farm Luwaks are deprived of a good combination of food items. In order to keep up with their health standards, it is important to allow civets to feed on the right combination of food items.

Chapter 3: Learning All About a Civet

While a number of businesses have already implemented the right habitat and feeding needs of the Luwaks, many of them are still not doing so in order to cut costs while producing more Kopi Luwak.

In the correct environment, the Farm Luwaks are provided with the best coffee beans to feed on, as well as the ripest fruits they are fond of. This helps them produce the best quality Kopi Luwak beans, as they do living in the forest and feeding on various different food items other than coffee berries.

Source:
http://upload.wikimedia.org/wikipedia/commons/2/28/Luwak-Katze_in_Kepahiang.jpg

The combination of food they eat, in addition to coffee berries, is the reason they are able to produce what we now call as the world's most expensive coffee available to date.

Primary Diet: Carnivore (eats eggs, insectivore, eats terrestrial vertebrates, eats non-insect arthropods, vermivore, molluscivore); herbivore (nectarivore, granivore, frugivore, folivore); omnivore.

Plant Food: Flowers; Nectar; Fruit; Nuts; Grains; Seeds; Sap and Fluids of other plants.

Animal Food: Smaller mammals; Birds; Amphibians; Eggs; Reptiles; Insects; Mollusks; Terrestrial non-insect arthropods; Terrestrial worms.

More Civets, More Coffee – The Mating process

Of course, the only way to produce more Kopi Luwak is to have more Kop Luwak producing Civets. Most Luwak farms in Indonesia pay to buy Luwaks for their farms. However, due to limited resources as well as the limited number of civets available in a region, it is not possible to own all the civets or majority of civets to be able to produce more Kopi Luwak and make more money.

Breeding and reproduction helped Luwak farms to multiply the number of Luwaks they own. Asian palm civets are secretive and nocturnal by nature and thus their reproductive behavior can only be observed when they are within a zoo or farm setting. Their mating system is also similar to that of cats. It is also known that civets typically give birth in tree hollows when in the wild as they are viviparous.

When in the wild, the Asian palm civets, that are known for their solitary characteristic, come together in the same trees for resting in order to mate for a continuous period between one and fifteen days. Luwaks find mates using their anal glands for scent marking, indicating the age, familiarity, kin relationship, receptivity and sex of each civet. As far as their sexual reception is concerned, they are active throughout the year with an average estrous cycle of eighty-two days. Typically, they have two litters in a year, giving birth from October to December.

In order to mate, they go into their resting trees. This is where they give birth and take care of their young ones, spending all this time from mating to giving birth in the tree of their choice. During the mating period, couples tend to keep close to other members of their species. They choose a tree that is in a close proximity to trees occupied by other members of their group.
After mating and spending the gestation period of 2 months together, Luwaks or Asian palm civets give birth to 2-5 kittens in boulder crevices or tree hollows for protection and secrecy.

The little kittens have their eyes closed and fur covering their bodies when they are born. The babies are very small, not weighing more than eighty grams at the time of birth. Only after eleven complete days do they open their eyes and by the time they turn two months old are weaned.

At the age of three months, little civets are considered fully grown and independent. However, until they turn one year old, they aren't sexually mature. As mentioned earlier, little is known about the sexual behavior and reproductive processes of civets due to their nocturnal and solitary habits. However, during March 2010, a palm civet couple was observed to understand their mating process and sexual behavior.

During the mating process, the male civet mounted the female 5-6 times. However, the pair separated and took breaks of about a few moments after each mounting. They repeated the same procedure several times.

Once the mating session was over, the couple frolicked around for a while, moving from one branch to another on the same tree. After about six minutes, the animals got separated and moved off to different branches to rest.

Similar observations are made for Farm Luwaks. During the mating session, the couple separated multiple times only to get back together to complete the mating session, after which, they moved separate ways to rest, even when they were within the same cage.

The female civet usually gives birth to her little ones on the preparations made by the people to welcome the new babies in the world. Of course, a litter of 2-5 babies is what will help the business flourish their Kopi Luwak business.

Taking Care of a Civet – What You Need to Know

There isn't a big difference in taking care of a baby and taking care of a young civet. Keeping Luwaks as a pet in a Luwak farm can be a wonderful experience altogether. However, you need to have a lot of patience to take care of civets in the best possible manner. Surprisingly, despite their solitary attitude, they enjoy being around humans and can quickly become comfortable in their new environment.

Things to consider

Of course, they are known for their scent glands and thus they do have an odor, which isn't very overwhelming. If you have a lot of civets caged in different areas around the farm, you will have to take extra care because the entire area can become very smelly.

Even if you raise the little babies as total pets, you can expect them to show their aggressive side. However, if you tackle them nicely and pay attention to their needs, you can simply inspire their aggression. Civets are not vicious animals, but when sad or upset, get yourself ready for a painful bite.

As mentioned before, they do have scent glands. Regarding how offensive their smell could be, it is totally subjective and a matter of personal preference.

When you have a farm loaded with Luwaks, make sure they are not startled, alarmed or upset by any of your acts if you do not want them to omit more odor.

Luwaks, when kept as pets on a farm, are sweet, playful and mischievous, provided they are treated in a nice way. Therefore, it is very important to take care of your civets, provide them with proper and sufficient food and take care of their living space, even if you decide to keep them in Luwak farms.

Whether you have civets as home pets or you have them on Luwak farms for business purposes, you are responsible to take care of this small mammal that is ready to adjust to a different habitat.

So provide them with different types of food, including coffee cherries if you have them for the purpose of producing Kopi Luwak. If you can, provide them with trees and other similar settings where they can jump, play and rest. Even give them a bowl of worms with sand where they can dig them up.

Bottom Line

By now, you have all the basic and important details about Civets and the rarest coffee they produce, Kopi Luwak. Read on to the next chapter to learn more about Kopi Luwak and how you can make the most out of every sip of this exotic coffee.

Chapter 4: Kopi Luwak on the Table

The exotic Kopi Luwak has been extracted, cleaned, washed and dried. The coffee beans have even gone through the roasting and packaging process. Now you have the world's most expensive coffee in your hands. What to do next? How to prepare a cup of coffee that you will remember for the rest of your life?

From preparing the perfect cup of Kopi Luwak to brewing and storage methods, there is much more you need to learn about Kopi Luwak in this chapter. So read on and make the most out of your 'Kopi Luwak cup of coffee' experience.

The Eight Rules to Making a Perfect Cup of Coffee

So now that you have your hands on the world's most expensive coffee, you want to make every sip of it count. Preparing a mesmerizing cup of Kopi Luwak at home does not require any rocket science. In fact, by keeping a few fundamental rules in mind, you can make the perfect Kopi Luwak coffee at home.

The coffee brewing equipment history is rich while the brewing methods are culturally dependent. Out of the hundreds of coffee brewing devices and machines invented since the advent of consumption of this desirable beverage, only a few gained international popularity.

The methods of brewing coffee given below are highly recommended to use when preparing Kopi Luwak coffee. Of course, this rare coffee has been found to increase the extraction of the coffee flavors on the whole. Follow the eight rules below and enjoy the perfect Kopi Luwak cup of joy.

Chapter 4: Kopi Luwak on the Table

Rule 1: Buy Some Good Coffee

It isn't possible to prepare some good coffee at home if you do not buy good coffee. Even when it comes to Kopi Luwak, you need to pay attention to the quality and authentication of the coffee you are purchasing. To get your hands on the best and most authentic Kopi Luwak coffee, first of all consider the most important factor, i.e. the rate at which the coffee goes stale and expires.

Of course, you will pay for the freshest available coffee. You must know that whole beans expire at a lower rate as compared to ground coffee. On the other hand, you need to pay attention to where you are buying your coffee, and take care to ensure that only quality coffee is bought from a high quality source.

Coffee is available in two ways: roasted and already ground or roasted in whole beans. A number of places offer you the convenience of buying coffee in the whole beans form and then grind them fresh on-site and take freshly ground coffee home. In short, if you want good coffee, you need to buy fresh coffee. Therefore, the basis for your decision to get the right coffee should be freshness and quality. Do not forget that coffee is a perishable consumable item and its expiry depends on its exposure to air. If it is longer in contact with the air, it will expire soon.

There is a possibility for the coffee to go stale if it is not kept airtight when not in use. Additionally, you must also remember that the deterioration rate of the coffee depends on whether the coffee is in whole beans or in ground form. Since grounding coffee beans breaks it down, there are chances it will go stale at a faster pace.

Thus, the piece of advice here is to buy Kopi Luwak in whole beans only and grind it at home whenever you need the world's best tasting cup of hot coffee. If you are worried about storing it for long, buy in small quantities only that is sufficient for a week or two and shop only when your first coffee storage is empty.

Also, make sure you keep your precious Kopi Luwak beans in an airtight jar to restrict exposure to air, sunlight and humidity to keep them safe for as long as possible.

For your knowledge, you must also know that the only type of coffee that does not expire or go stale within days of exposure to sunlight and air is the unroasted, green coffee beans.

Believe it or not, unroasted, raw green coffee beans can be kept for years, and the only time they will expire is once they are roasted to brown. The most authentic sellers of Kopi Luwak around the world roast this most expensive and rarest coffee only when they receive orders from buyers to keep it safe for as long as they can.

Rule 2: Coffee Beans Should Not Be Stored in the Refrigerator

A lot of people believe that by storing their coffees in the freezer or fridge, like many other things, will keep the coffee in its original form for longer. Coffee, unlike other perishable things that can be kept frozen to last longer, is an exception. Have you ever seen a refrigerator or any other cold storage place in any coffee shop? No coffee stores or coffee cafes store their priceless coffee in a refrigerator.

As mentioned before, humidity is bad for the quality of your coffee. Even if you have coffee beans, they might stick together due to humidity, thus reducing the quality. The fact that the change in temperatures experienced by coffee beans from room temperature to temperature below 0 degree Celsius (32 degree Fahrenheit) and back to the room temperature for brewing will result in 'condensation', thus introducing humidity, that's bad for the longevity of the coffee.

Eventually, the 'condensation' will cause the humidity to leave when the coffee beans congeal, and together with it, much of its freshness and flavor. This is something absolutely unacceptable when it comes to Kopi Luwak, which is not only highly priced but known for its unique taste and incredible flavor.

On the other hand, even warm temperature is not ideal when it comes to storing your precious Kopi Luwak coffee beans. In short, in order to keep them in the best possible form, store them in an airtight jar at room temperature and keep them in a dark, dry place. This is the easiest and most effective way to keep the precious coffee beans from going stale.

Rule 3: Brew in Fresh, Clean Water Only

What's coffee? To be very honest, it is nothing more than flavored water. The medium to make Coffee is mostly plain water. In fact, it is revealed that almost 99 percent of coffee is water and the remaining 1 percent is the flavor of coffee.

In order to prepare a good cup of coffee, you need to use fresh and clean water only. If you begin the brewing process with water that is unclean or tastes bad, do not expect your coffee to taste good. If you are using tap water loaded with chlorine, the flavor of your coffee will automatically dampen. It is not the water that has to taste strong, even treated water can destroy the taste of your coffee.

When it comes to Kopi Luwak, it is a luxury coffee that one tries for the sake of enjoying taste and flavor that are regarded as 'out of this world.' If you prepare this luxury coffee in tap water or water that tastes funny, you will destroy your 'out of this world' coffee experience.

Similarly, well water loaded with various dissolved minerals will not let the flavors of your coffee shine at its best. Thus, the idea here is to use clean, flavorless, filtered water to get the best out of your Kopi Luwak brew and experience.

Rule 4: Use Hot Water Only!

If you are a beginner brewer, you might overlook this one. It is important to remember that water temperature is crucial if you want to extract maximum flavors from those exotic coffee beans. To tell you from my own experience, coffees brewed at 80°C (176°F), 90°C (194° F), and 99° C (210° F) are absolutely different and are so dramatic that one can immediately recognize them, even if he or she is a casual coffee consumer.

In fact, the difference is sometimes so dramatic and obvious that it can become challenging to figure out whether the coffee brewed at different temperatures were made from the same beans or not.

Optimum temperature for water for brewing Kopi Luwak is 95° C (203° F) plus or minus two percent. If the water is hotter than this, you might end up with an astringent, bitter tasting coffee. On the other hand, if the water is cool and below the ideal temperature, the coffee will taste completely flat. The ideal way to go about it is to boil water on high medium-high flame and then turn off the heat and allow it to cool briefly for not more than 50 second before adding coffee and brewing it.

Rule 5: The Ideal Coffee-Water Ratio

For a perfect coffee, you need to follow the perfect coffee-water ratio. No matter in which direction the ratio is off, you will taste the world's most exotic coffee and probably will not enjoy it or find it naturally different.

In order to achieve the right balance between coffee and water, you first need to begin with the appropriate measurement of ground coffee sufficient for the amount of water you will be using.

Get yourself a standard coffee measuring scoop. One scoop is usually equivalent to two tablespoons (levelled). To be specific, 9 grams of ground coffee is ideal to prepare 17ml (6 oz.) of water. The scoop method is usually preferred because it takes you closer to achieving the ideal coffee-water balance. Of course, once you are close to the ideal proportions, you can fine-tune the flavors according to your taste.

Rule 6: Adjust the Grind Setting Right

Now that you have learnt how to adjust the perfect balance between coffee and water ratio, the next thing you need to pay attention to is the right grind setting. Indeed, correcting your coffee and water ratio is not enough when you are after the perfect cup of Kopi Luwak coffee.

Pay attention to the grind setting because after all what is extracted counts. The taste of Kopi Luwak coffee is controlled by the association between how it is grinded and how the ground coffee comes in contact with the boiling water.

The grind used for brewing should be in accordance with the brewing time as well as the brewing method. Coffee that is too coarsely ground doesn't provide sufficient surface area, leading to a weak-testing, under-extracted brew.

On the other hand, if the grind is too thin and fine, the coffee is over-extracted due to the wide surface area. Such coffee usually tastes bitter and flavorless.

The grind for different types of brewing methods is given in the table below:

Brewing Method	Grind
Drip	Medium
French Press	Coarse
Moka Pots (Espresso)	Fine

For home use, you can choose from the two main and most common coffee bean grinders: the coffee mill (also known as the burr grinder) and bladed grinder.

The burr grinder or coffee mill grinds the coffee beans using two different serrated discs or burrs. First of all, you choose the type of grind according to your preference, add the coffee beans into the chamber, and turn it on to start grinding.

Eventually, the coffee beans will grind and the next chamber will be filled with ground coffee that is ready to be brewed instantly. The best part about this grinder is that the grind is absolutely consistent. Sadly, this isn't used widely.

On the other hand you have the whirling-blade grinder. This is more common and popular amongst the people. This grinder has two-sided single blade that rotates and chops the coffee beans at once. Load the beans into the chamber and turn it on to begin grinding. Unfortunately, there is no speed or time setting that will give you consistent results every time you grind. Thus, based on your personal experience, you will operate the grinder manually.

You can have a look at the ground coffee from the top of the transparent grinder cover. Stop whenever you think it is done according to your preference. You can give it another spin if you are not satisfied with the results.

Unfortunately, you will not receive a consistent grind using this method and potentially ruin the entire grinding experience since there are no specific grind settings.

Then why do people use it? First, it is a very common grinder that is easy to afford and convenient to find. Second, it still does the job after all. All in all, if you are looking for consistency, go for burr grinder to get the best coffee grinding experience.

Rule 7: Cleanliness is the Key!

Don't forget, coffee is very oily. You need to pay special attention to the overall cleanliness if you want to enjoy the perfect cup of the luxurious Kopi Luwak coffee.

At a first glance, the coffee may look pretty dry. However, they are naturally very oily and unless you completely clean and dry all the equipment for brewing, these coffee oils will become rancid and can spoil future brews, resulting in a bad, sour taste.

Clean everything that comes in contact with the luxury coffee beans you paid a fortune for a single cup. Preferably, clean the equipment with warm water and soap after each use. Don't forget to disassemble the brewer, if applicable, and scrub it thoroughly for best results.

Rule 8: Once Brewed, Do Not Reheat

At 80° C (176° F), brewed Kopi Luwak coffee will taste its best. This is the temperature where the chemical compounds, which are responsible for making coffee flavorful, are at the most stable form. In order to achieve this, decant the Kopi Luwak brewed coffee into a carafe or thermos that has been preheated with the help of simple boiled water.

It is important to preheat the containers or your exotic brew will lose the required heat as soon as it is poured into container with a different temperature altogether.

If you are directly serving them in mugs, make sure you preheat the mugs to adjust the temperature of the mugs according to the coffee. However, the idea of using heating plates to keep the mug heated will not work here. The continuous heat affects the taste and can impart bitter or burnt flavors.

In short, if you really want to enjoy that exotic cup of Kopi Luwak, do not let it sit for more than 15 minutes. The sooner you will consume it, the better idea you will have about its natural, rare and unique taste.

These 8 rules will make your Kopi Luwak experience at home worth the money spent. If you are trying Kopi Luwak for the first time and are risking preparing it at home, these 8 rules will save you from the disasters many beginners make.

More importantly, most of these rules apply to all types of coffee in addition to Kopi Luwak. So regardless of which coffee you have in hand, applying these 8 rules will definitely impact your coffee drinking experience in a very positive way.

Serve the Coffee Right

The most expensive coffee in the world deserves to be served right. Therefore, you need to learn the best and most popular brewing methods that will help you prepare the best Kopi Luwak coffee ever. In addition to the methods mentioned below, there are other methods like, The Percolator, The Vacuum Pot, The Cold Brewing and The Ibrik (Turkish coffee). However, I will focus on the more popular and convenient methods that will enhance your overall Kopi Luwak brewing experience.

The Moka Pot (The Stovetop Espresso Maker)

Do you want to enjoy a dark, flavorful and strong Kopi Luwak coffee? If yes, then the Moka Pot brewing method is perfect for you. If you want your coffee to be as strong as those conventional espresso makers produce, then try this Italian steam-based stovetop espresso maker known as the Moka Pot.

Introduced by Alfonso Bialetti during the year 1933, the Moka Pot espresso makers are popular to date. However, in the true sense of the word, the coffee is different from the real espresso, which is produced with the help of a machine that produces water at very high pressure according to the right temperature. MokaPot coffee, however, is produced only by using the natural pressure of steam.

Moka Pots are named as such because it comprises of three metal pots. These three-chambered pots are available from 2 to 12 cups sizes.

1. First, there is a bottom metal chamber to hold fresh water. This pot generally has a pressure valve installed.
2. The next one is the middle pot, which is a perforated funnel or coffee basket to hold the coffee grounds. Make sure the grounds are lightly packed in this chamber.

3. The last chamber, which adjusts on the top, is the pot where you get your prepared, brewed Kopi Luwak coffee.

In this brewing method, fill the bottom chamber with clean water (hot or cold, as you desire) up to the valve. Next, set the funnel pot. Now add ground Kopi Luwak in this chamber and level it thoroughly. Make sure you do not tamp or pack it.

Source:
http://upload.wikimedia.org/wikipedia/commons/thumb/8/89/Moka_Pezzetti_per_alimenti_08.jpg/768px-Moka_Pezzetti_per_alimenti_08.jpg

If you believe there are residues in the brew, it is preferable if you grind the coffee beans using a coarse grinder. Next, the two halves should be screwed together tightly. Set the Moka Pot over the stove and set the heat to low-medium flame.

Automatically, the coffee will start flowing to the top-most metal pot. After around 5 minutes, your exotic Kopi Luwak will start to sputter. If it is taking longer than 5 minutes, adjust the heat a bit higher. Once the coffee starts to sputter, turn off the heat, and remove the Moka pot from the stove. Stir for a few seconds before you serve the most expensive, exotic coffee in the world to your taste buds. Congratulations, you are holding the luxurious cup of coffee in your hand that many others can only think of.

Now, time to clean the equipment! You should never put the Moka Pot in a dishwasher to clean. Use water and mild detergent to wash the pots and then dry thoroughly using a clean cloth after each wash. It is important that you keep your Moka pot clean at all times. After using it, disassemble the pots and clean the top pot and filters too. Also, make sure you clean the underside of each pot before after each use.

Moka pots require extra care when it comes to cleanliness. If you want to have the same, incredible Kopi Luwak experience every time, make sure you take care of the equipment too. Moka pots also require some vinegar treatment, i.e. clean Moka pot with some vinegar as if you were brewing coffee. This process will help you remove any unyielding mineral deposits left behind.

It is important to note here that the amount of coffee an individual Moka pot makes depends on its size. The Moka pot specifies the set amount of coffee it will prepare. Do not try to make less Kopi Luwak by not filling the basket sufficiently. On the other hand, do not even try to make more coffee by compacting too tightly or over-filling the pot.

Doing so will affect the process of extraction and will result in either weak or bitter coffee. Instead, you should buy an appropriately sized Moka pot that matches your requirement of the number of cups you want to brew.

French Press

Experts suggest that brewing your Kopi Luwak coffee using the French Press brewing method is the single best way to prepare your coffee. This is because this method of preparing Kopi Luwak allows prolonged and direct contact between coffee and water without actually boiling the coffee.

Source: http://farm4.staticflickr.com/3147/2620250456_7dc5107323_o.jpg

This method also uses every piece of the ground coffee and you will not find any remaining at the bottom of your coffee cup. The following is a guide that will help you with this method efficiently.

1. First of all, heat water on the stove at low-medium flame.

2. In case you do not have ground Kopi Luwak coffee, grind it using the preferred method to a coarse grind. There are two reasons to coarse grind. First, to ensure the solids are not over-extracted from the coffee and second to make sure the

coffee is not finely ground that it easily passes through the filter.

3. Adjust the French Press coffee maker and set in the ground coffee. The French Press coffee maker is a large, simple glass container.

4. Once the water starts to boils, turn the heat off and remove from the stove. Let the water sit for a minute so that the temperature adjusts. You need to use hot water, not boiling water. Now add the hot water to the container with the coffee. Don't forget to keep the coffee-water ratio right to brew the best tasting coffee in the best possible manner. For instance, if you are preparing two cups of Kopi Luwak coffee, pour only two cups of hot water in the French Press container.

5. Use a plastic spoon to stir the mixture. Cover the container with the plunger and the lid pulled up to the top.

6. Allow the mixture to sit for a few minutes. Adjust the flavors according to personal taste and try it several times.

7. Now bring the plunger down until it makes its way all the way to the bottom. The ground coffee will be pushed down and will be pressed to the bottom when you push the plunger.

8. Time to try the brewed Kopi Luwak! Pour the coffee from the French Press container. Automatically, the filter will separate the brewed coffee and the coffee grinds so that you only get pure, brewed coffee.

9. Your perfect cup of Kopi Luwak is now in your hand. The best tasting and the world's most expensive coffee is ready and served to treat your taste buds.

10. Make sure you clean up the French Press container after each use. To clean, remove the plunger and lid first. Clean the remaining ground coffee first and dump it in the garbage. Rinse the plunger and the lift thoroughly in clean water and don't forget to clean the glass Fresh Press container with clean water and mild soap.

Drip Brewers (Manual Coffee Maker)

In contrast to automatic drip coffee makers, many people still prefer this time honored, manual drip coffee making tradition using the Drip Brewers. This tradition is often preferred due to the fact that manual drip coffee makers allow the brewers to have great control over extraction maintenance.

The water is heated separately and simply poured over the grounds of exotic Kopi Luwak coffee at a desirable pace. Depending on your taste preference, you can prepare a very strong Kopi Luwak coffee without worrying about the spills that are a normal occurrence in automatic coffee makers. You can add more grounds of Kopi Luwak coffee and make your coffee as strong as you like.

The best way to prepare your Kopi Luwak coffee is to first add the coffee grounds and then pour over boiling water sufficient enough to cover the coffee grounds. This will make the flavor of the coffee bloom. Once the first session of water disappears in the coffee grounds, pour more water, this time keeping the level of water right above the grounds.

If you really want to enjoy a pleasing cup of Kopi Luwak, make sure you are very accurate and consistent with the measurement of coffee grounds. You should even measure water before heating it. This will save you from accidentally pouring extra water onto the grounds.

Chapter 4: Kopi Luwak on the Table

Once your perfect cup of Kopi Luwak is brewed, hold the coffee pot in your hand and swirl it to give it a final stir. Very few people are aware of the fact that coffee that is poured first through the filter into the carafe is comparatively stronger than the coffee that drips at the end of the cycle.

Source:
http://upload.wikimedia.org/wikipedia/commons/9/92/Manual_coffee_preperation.jpg

The filter type you are using in this manual method also holds great significance. You have two distinctive choices: a filter made of paper that is easily available at a coffee aisle on the local grocery store, or a filter made of metal that is re-usable after thorough cleaning after each brewing session.

Chapter 4: Kopi Luwak on the Table

As far as a paper filter is concerned, a number of people prefer this method since it is disposable. You simply pull the paper filter out and through the ground coffee residue in the garbage. In short, no cleaning is required in this one.

However, there is something you lose for the sake of convenience. A paper filter absorbs colloids that if allowed to pass through would result in a more delicious, full-bodied coffee. Colloid is nothing but coffee that is fully brewed. Of course, it does not get dissolved but adds body to your coffee.

The paper filter traps the colloid. On the other hand, people who are aware of this fact prefer a metal filter. A metal filter allows colloid to pass through and add body to your cup of coffee.

This is the reason why coffee that is brewed using a metal filter results in sediments deep down in your cup. If you think sediment is a bad thing, remember, it is not! It is just leftover solids of the coffee extracted from coffee grounds that paper filters do not allow to pass.

So the choice between filters is absolutely personal. If you want fuller body coffee and make your lifetime Kopi Luwak experience worthwhile, go for a metal filter and if you wish to avoid the mess, just grab those disposable paper filters.

The Best Way to Store Your Coffee

Like storing regular coffee, Kopi Luwak storage is rife with poor practices and misconceptions. The fact that this coffee is extremely expensive and very scarce in supply, people who pay to get this exotic coffee cannot afford to lose even a single bean or a teaspoon of ground Kopi Luwak.

While experts recommend roasting Kopi Luwak beans only when you want to consume it immediately, many people purchase roasted (and even ground) coffee available at authentic stores. If it is in bulk, you cannot expect an individual to prepare all the coffee at once.
Therefore, it is very important to learn how to store Kopi Luwak beans as well as ground coffee at its best for maximum flavor and freshness.

What to Avoid?

To put it straight, the following are four things you need to keep your coffee safe from:

- Heat
- Moisture
- Light
- Air

Locations for Storing Kopi Luwak

- Dry, dark and cool places are the right places to store your worthy coffee beans. Such places include cabinets and pantries. These are the best places for Kopi Luwak storage.

- As mentioned earlier in the book, Kopi Luwak should never be stored in freezers and fridges. These two places are moist and can ruin your coffee. However, there are a few exceptions when it comes to freezing Kopi Luwak beans. We will discuss it in detail below.

- Avoid storing your coffee in warm spots, such as near a flame or oven or in cabinets with high temperature.

- Use only airtight storage vessels to save your coffee from coming in direct contact with air. Once stored in airtight vessels, coffee can be placed on open countertops that are far away from all sources of heat, including sunlight.

Types of Coffee Containers for Storage

Coffee loses its freshness the moment its original packaging is opened. As far as reserving the freshness and flavors of Kopi Luwak is concerned, non-reactive metal, ceramic or glass containers with airtight gaskets are the best containers for storing your luxury coffee.

Store your coffee fresh in a clear plastic or glass ware only if you will be storing the canisters in a dark, cool place. If you want to display the storage on the countertop, airtight, opaque containers are ideal.

The Freshness of Your Kopi Luwak Overtime

As you know, roasting plays an important part in giving Kopi Luwak the taste and flavors it is known for. However, once the beans are roasted, coffee begins to lose its freshness. The peak days are soon after Kopi Luwak is roasted.

This is the reason why experts suggest coffee connoisseurs to opt for green, unroasted coffee beans instead of roasted coffee grounds.
As far as ground Kopi Luwak coffee is concerned, it should not be stored for more than two weeks if you really want to know why Kopi

Chapter 4: Kopi Luwak on the Table

Luwak is unique, different and the most exotic and luxurious coffee in the world.

The real magic of Kopi Luwak keeps decreasing as it goes from one process to the other. Until the coffee is roasted and ground, it has been through all the possible processes before brewing. This is the point where you need to consume your coffee as soon as possible to enjoy the unique, incredible taste of Kopi Luwak.

To keep your roasted coffee fresh, buy coffee that is just roasted. There are many retailers who offer that service. You buy the green beans and they will roast it for you according to your preference. If you are a buying a few pounds of Kopi Luwak for storage, make sure you store the bulk in an airtight, tightly sealed container and keep it in a dark, cool area. For regular use, keep smaller quantities in a smaller container separately.

You will only need to open the larger container when the smaller one needs to be refilled. Other than that, for your daily or regular use, you can store coffee in a smaller container. This will reduce exposure to air and moisture.

Freshness of Whole Beans vs. Ground Kopi Luwak

Since the surface area of ground coffee is more than whole beans, there are increased chances for it to go bad much faster. Kopi Luwak is known for its exclusivity in production, extraction, taste and flavors. Thus, it is more sensitive to external factors than any other coffee. Allowing exposure to heat, light, air and moisture can destroy the unique flavor and taste completely and can make this incredible, exotic coffee nothing more than a regular coffee.

Therefore, you must pay special attention to maintaining the freshness of this one.

- Kopi Luwak whole beans should ideally be consumed within three to four weeks of roasting. Since the production and packaging takes place in different regions of Asia, the exotic coffee is exported to different international regions. When investing in the world's most expensive coffee, make sure it isn't very old, especially if it is roasted.

- If you are buying roasted ground Kopi Luwak coffee, consume it within a week or two of roasting.

- To enhance the taste and flavors of your Kopi Luwak coffee beans, grind them at home just before you are ready to brew.

Green Beans

Yes, you can even buy green beans of Kopi Luwak. A number of retailers in Indonesia are selling clean green Kopi Luwak beans to the international market. You can buy a pound (around 450 grams) of green beans that you can roast at home and grind before using.

This is indeed the best way to enjoy the most authentic Kopi Luwak taste. However, due to convenience, people often choose to buy processed and ready-to-be-brewed coffee.

- Green Kopi Luwak coffee beans are available at various coffee retailers both offline and online.

- Green beans are a preferred option because they store much longer and better than coffee beans that are roasted. If green beans are roasted using the roasting methods outlined above and are stored in the most ideal manner, you can keep them fresh for more than a year. Of course, it does not require rocket science to roast green coffee at home or to grind them according to your own personal preferences.

- Soon after you roast Kopi Luwak coffee at home, the beans will retain lots of carbon dioxide. The best way is to store the roasted beans in an airtight container or a valve-sealed bag (discussed below) and access it at least once every day for several days for a few seconds to release the accumulated carbon dioxide.

Freeze It Up!

Yes, in some situations, freezing is an available option. But when? When you are importing your favorite Kopi Luwak from its native land, Indonesia in bulk and you know you will not be using it for the next few weeks.

Yes, coffee stays fresh for no more than two weeks and if you do not have any plans to use all of the coffee within this time frame, better freeze the excess coffee. You can pull out a small container of coffee that you will be using on a regular basis; the rest would go in the freezer.

However, that is not a permanent solution. It is acceptable but only as a temporary one. This means that once you take your coffee beans out of the freezer, you will never put them back in again. The continuous change in the temperature is bad for your coffee.

When you remove the beans from the freezer, the moisture will melt and absorb in the beans. If you repeat the process and put it back in, the absorbed moisture will destroy the flavors and taste completely.

The main aim behind freezing coffee beans is to store its freshness and keep it away from moisture. Thus, you should divide the coffee you want to store and use very carefully. So if you have ordered coffee that could be used in 4 weeks, divide it into weekly portions.

After dividing the portions, pack them in sealable freezer bags and then wrap it up with plastic wraps before placing them in the freezer. Now remove only one pack for a week and store it in a preferable, air tight container and never put it back in the freezer again.

Refrigerating Coffee

Putting coffee in the refrigerator is a big No-No! Never refrigerate your Kopi Luwak beans or grounds unless you want to ruin the coffee completely and waste your money. The fridge is the worst place to store this coffee.

Valve-Sealed and Vacuum-Sealed Coffees

- Before coffee is vacuum-sealed, it is allowed to age. If freshly roasted coffee is vacuum-sealed, the gases will be released by the coffee as it loses freshness and can cause the package to expand even make it burst open.

- Vacuum-sealed coffee is not intended for home storage. In fact, it is a type of packaging, intended for supermarkets and grocery store shelves. Also, the coffee is considered to be of lower quality as compared to freshly-roasted coffee.

- On the other hand, you have a valve-sealed package that allows the gases to escape from the packaging and at the same time does not let any external gases enter the packaging. This packaging method is more convenient as it allows you to immediately store the coffee soon after roasting.

- Comparatively, valve-sealed coffee is considered much better and fresher than coffee packed in a vacuum-sealed package. But if you are after the best and most incredible flavor of Kopi Luwak, try the fresh, ground coffee only.

- There are limitations associated with valve and vacuum sealed coffees as well. Even they lose their quality within a week or two after they are opened.

More on Kopi Luwak

Here we will share a few facts about Kopi Luwak to cover some more information and to give a quick recap on whatever we have learned.

1. Just like other regular coffees, Kopi Luwak or civet coffee is designed for immediate consumption. The sooner you give this exotic coffee a try, the more you enjoy it's incredible, unique taste. Two weeks for ground coffee and four weeks for roasted beans are more than enough.

2. Kopi Luwak originally comes from various Asian origins. Indonesia, Vietnam and Philippine are, however, on top of the list. Oprah Winfrey defined the unique coffee from the Sumatra Islands, Indonesia, as the best coffee ever on her show.

3. Real Kopi Luwak is rich, more syrupy and has a full body characteristic. It has a natural chocolaty, caramel-like taste. The aroma of the coffee is extremely strong too, making coffee connoisseurs crazy about it.

Bottom Line

Before you invest in an expensive cup of Kopi Luwak coffee, make sure you are buying it from an authentic place. Also, you should know how to differentiate between fake and real Kopi Luwak. This is discussed in more detail later in the book.

Some more relevant information could be found on this site:
http://www.kopiluwakcoffeefacts.com/

Keep reading!

Chapter 4: Kopi Luwak on the Table

Chapter 5: The Unique Characteristics

Kopi Luwak is popular because of its unique characteristics. There is much more to this coffee than its unconventional source of production that makes it very irresistable. This includes the natural, unique harvesting techniques and the fermentation techniques that profoundly impact the taste, flavor and quality of each and every coffee bean.

Disclosing the General Properties of Kopi Luwak Coffee

Characteristics of popular civet coffee also include its smooth taste, strong aroma, natural chocolaty and caramel-like flavors, and low acidity. And of course, the unique production and extraction method since Kopi Luwak is made with coffee beans that are retrieved from a civet's excretion.

The unique aroma and taste of Kopi Luwak are the main reasons this exotic coffee has gained immense popularity despite the off-putting information that the coffee is initially excreted by a small animal. It is indeed disgusting for a number of people to learn that the excrement is gathered and goes through different processes to prepare a cup of special coffee.

An authentic civet coffee is quite heavy, full bodied and has a syrupy texture. It has a natural pleasant sweetness that reveals hints of subtle caramel and chocolate taste. The flavors of Kopi Luwak coffee are complex with low acidity and bitterness levels. The complex flavors and rich aroma gives your perfect cup of Kopi Luwak a smooth finish as well as an aftertaste that is clean and long.

Chapter 5: The Unique Characteristics

As far as quality is concerned, it is believed that civet coffee produced in different Asian regions and made from different quality of coffee plants will definitely result in distinctly different qualities. However, it is a common factor among all qualities of Kopi Luwak that it is rich, smooth and naturally sweet, which is why it does not require heavy roasting.

The common Sumatran Kopi Luwak is known to have a lighter body with bright beans and persistent finish. Kopi Luwak produced in different regions have their own distinct aromas and flavors. Also, the variation will occur depending on whether the coffee is produced by wild civets (that are allowed to choose the coffee berries themselves), or Kopi Luwak produced by farm civets that are provided the coffee berries by the caretakers.

Roasted civet coffee of fine quality is allowed to exhibit its premium gourmet qualities and unique origin flavors, which are very prominent since the flavors are not covered by dark roasting.

This results in an aromatic, smooth, and very pleasant tasting cup of brewed coffee that naturally reveals hints of various nuanced flavors, including coffee and caramel. When brewed smoothly, the coffee is also said to reveal distinctive oaky and nutty flavors that cannot be found in other coffees.

How to Distinguish the Real One from the Fake

The supply of Kopi Luwak is extremely scarce. The rarity factor is the main reason Kopi Luwak is sold for such a high price. To be able to sell Kopi Luwak is more like an opportunity; a one-off chance to make a lot of money. And people around the world wanted to make the most out of this opportunity; some with real Kopi Luwak while others with fake ones.

I want to warn you that more than 70 percent of Kopi Luwak coffee available on the internet as well as on local coffee stores is not 100 percent pure Kopi Luwak and at times does not even contain anything that is associated with genuine Kopi Luwak coffee.

Sadly, there is no certification that can guarantee that you are investing in a real, worthwhile Kopi Luwak coffee. Thus, your expertise and your ability to distinguish the real ones from the fake can help you enjoy the real taste of the exotic Kopi Luwak.

Tips That Will Save You from Fake Kopi Luwak

There are a few things you need to watch out for. Beware of the following and apply your judgement:

Low Prices

Authentic Kopi Luwak is never available at cheap rates. If it is real, it has to be expensive. People offering Kopi Luwak that is not 100 percent genuine or are completely fake, often try to sell what they have at a lower price, catching people's attention with their extremely low rates.

Kopi Luwak is scarce and produces around 700kg to 800kg in a year. This is the main reason for its high prices. Be very careful with blended Kopi Luwak. If you want to enjoy the experience of real Kopi

Luwak, do not invest in any product that claims to be the blended form of the unique civet coffee. It is difficult to analyze the percentage of Kopi Luwak added to a regular coffee blend. Sometimes the percentage can be as low as 1 percent, while at other times, nothing!

You will notice that the price of blended product is far less than the price of real Kopi Luwak. A little research about the current price of this quality coffee will help you in this.

Guarantees

Never accept it as a real Kopi Luwak even if there is a guarantee attached of a famous coffee gourmet. Not a lot of people have had the privilege of tasting the genuine civet coffee, therefore it is pretty difficult to distinguish and compare aroma, taste, acidity and body of the coffee. Do not believe such guarantees because nobody is able to guarantee if the coffee is actually and 100 percent Kopi Luwak simply by tasting it.

Wholesale

Since Kopi Luwak is a scarce coffee, selling this product for bulk or massive consumption does not seem possible unless the product contains just a low percentage of genuine Kopi Luwak beans.

Certificate

Unfortunately, there is no official certificate to guarantee authentic coffee released by any official government to date. Some sellers, however, provide a different type of certificate that comes from independent research institutions which does not certify the originality of Kopi Luwak, rather clarify about the result compound of the coffee beans, such as fragrance, taste, moisture, uniformity, etc. Therefore, it does not prove the authenticity by any means.

How to Differentiate Between Ordinary Beans and Kopi Luwak Beans

1. The unroasted green beans of Kopi Luwak coffee smell like pandan leaf. The fragrance of the fake one has a smell that resembles that of rice.

2. The color of all green Luwak beans is the same. It is more of a yellowish green shade than a pure green. You will not find such uniformity in fake ones.

3. The shape of a real Kopi Luwak coffee bean is pretty good. There are no black spots in the structure of the bean. Also, there is no broken structure in the real Kopi Luwak beans since the civets are known for eating the ripest and best coffee berries. Fake ones have very prominent broken structures.

4. The aftertaste of pure Luwak coffee lingers on the tongue for longer. It is very syrupy, full in body and very rich. Authentic coffee has a very strong aroma, much stronger than ordinary coffee. However, the cupping differentiation can only be observed after trying a cup of coffee that claims to be original Kopi Luwak.

5. Ulcer patients who are sensitive to coffee can also help you differentiate the real one from the fake. Luwak coffee does not harm ulcer patients. If an ulcer patient drinks Luwak coffee and does not experience a relapse, consider the coffee authentic. This method is however risky and not recommended.

Where to Find It?

Don't worry; this book will not end without giving you information about places where you can find the most authentic Kopi Luwak coffee.

While many people would recommend you to fly all the way to Indonesia to get your hands on the most authentic Kopi Luwak coffee, right from the farms where they are produced, that's probably too much to do.

The cost of Kopi Luwak is pretty high in itself and then adding additional costs of travelling all the way to Kopi Luwak's native islands does not seem a very good idea. Unless, of course, if you are planning a business trip or a leisure holiday.

When you have authentic Kopi Luwak available in your own country and city, you can simply eliminate the hassle and enjoy the most incredible coffee drinking experience with Kopi Luwak.

Yes that is right. With a number of retailers fooling people and selling fake coffee under the name of Kopi Luwak, there are places you can find authentic Kopi Luwak within your city and country. So whether you are in USA, UK, Indonesia, Singapore, Hong Kong, Canada or Australia, you can buy original and authentic Kopi Luwak both online and offline. You can enjoy more details on this in the next chapter.

Cost Analysis – Why Kopi Luwak Is the World's Most Expensive Coffee?

The complex process of preparing Kopi Luwak coffee and the way this coffee is produced is the main reason behind its high prices. As mentioned earlier in the book, Kopi Luwak is not only unique but extremely rare, making it the scarcest coffee in the world.

Currently, Kopi Luwak can cost you around 90 US dollars per cup (55 GBP). If you are asked to pay such a high price for a single cup of regular coffee, you will definitely say a big 'No'. But you cannot compare Kopi Luwak to any regular coffee.

The idea sounds crazy to many in the beginning. Coffee beans that are produced and extracted from animal faeces actually make up the most expensive coffee in the world. However, it is just a matter of a single sip and you will change your perception immediately.

It has a rather 'otherworldly' taste that will have a magical effect on you. The strong aroma and sweet, smooth taste of the world's best tasting coffee will weave a spell on you and you will not be able to stop yourself from trying it.

The other way to enjoy this expensive coffee is to purchase a few pounds of these exquisite coffee beans. Of course, that will be pretty expensive, but then you will have more of Kopi Luwak to enjoy at a relatively low price per cup. Coffee connoisseurs do not hesitate in spending on Kopi Luwak and if you are one of them, you won't either.

Still wondering what makes this coffee so special and luxurious? Indeed, the labor involved in the process of developing Kopi Luwak into a consumable commodity ups the price. Other than this, any commodity cannot be priced so high and extravagantly unless and until it offers something that satisfies the senses; Kopi Luwak satisfies your craving for an exotic coffee by serving your taste buds.

No wonder this coffee was highly glorified on The Oprah Winfrey Show! With increasing popularity, this rare coffee is now expected to reach a broader audience. So if you are ready to put your hands on the world's most expensive and highest quality coffee, Kopi Luwak it is!

Bottom Line

The next chapter will reveal the best and most authentic places to order your Kopi Luwak, within your county. Keep reading!

Chapter 6: Around the World for Kopi Luwak

Native to the Indonesian Islands, original Kopi Luwak is now available in different parts of the world. This chapter covers all important details that you need in order to get the best and most authentic Kopi Luwak within your country.

Information on distributors, sellers and shops in different cities in the UK, USA, Indonesia, Singapore, Hong Kong, Canada and Australia can be found here. Just go to your nearby coffee store, Kopi Luwak coffee shop, seller or distributor and enjoy the most exotic cup of Kopi Luwak coffee.

Finding the Right Place to Buy Kopi Luwak

Indeed, finding the rarest coffee within your city or country is challenging, especially if it is produced at the other end of the world. Kopi Luwak is native to Indonesia and thus, many people believe that finding the most authentic Kopi Luwak is only possible within that region.

To some extent, this information is right. I know a lot of people who have actually travelled all the way to Indonesia and Sumatra Island to try the cup of the most exotic coffee in the world. However, not everyone has that luxury, do they?

Plus the business opportunities that rose with the advent of Kopi Luwak could not be overlooked. People around the world were curious to find out more about this coffee and make the most out of the opportunities available to them. A number of people invested in

Kopi Luwak, and brought it all the way from Indonesia to their native countries and offered them to people at a higher price.

Even today, people around the world import Kopi Luwak from Indonesia and other Asian local civet coffee producers and sell it for a much higher price.

Fortunately, with people dealing in the world's most expensive coffee within your country, you do not have to visit Indonesia to try coffee that people can only think of. So if you find the price worth trying the rarest and most exotic coffee in the world, do not hesitate in trying out your luck in the coffee shops and coffee companies mentioned in the book below to enjoy the experience of life.

Do You Need a License to Sell Kopi Luwak in USA, UK, Australia and Other Countries?

Surprisingly, no! A special license is not required to sell Kopi Luwak. In fact, you need a license to run a coffee business and that includes any coffee. If you have a coffee café or a restaurant, you will need a license to run your business legally anyway. There are no exceptions for Kopi Luwak.

However, some countries impose legalities, rules and regulations on importing Kopi Luwak from Indonesia. For instance, an individual without a licensed business in Australia cannot import Kopi Luwak with the intentions of selling it. That would be regarded as being illegal.

To be able to import in Australia, you need to know the following conditions. An Import Permit is not required for civet coffee/Kopi Luwak, including ground, whole beans, or coffee ready-for use, provided that:

1. The coffee beans or grounds are roasted; and
2. The coffee is prepared and packaged commercially; and
3. Imported not less than 1 liter (prepared) or 1 kilogram; and
4. Is only imported for personal use.

Similarly, there are different outlines for different countries that you need to check on a current basis, in case you are planning to import some for yourself all the way from Indonesia.

However, if you are looking forward to avoid that hassle, I can help you here. Below I have listed places in the UK, USA, Indonesia, Singapore, Hong Kong, Canada and Australia, where they offer you a hot, sizzling cup of Kopi Luwak. You can also get roasted beans and ground Kopi Luwak coffee at many coffee cafés listed below.

Places to turn to for Kopi Luwak experience include the following:

UK

1. DSTRKT London, Rupert Street, London, UK

Website: http://www.yaneffatdstrkt.co.uk/

Address:
9 Rupert Street,
London, W1D 6DG, UK

Phone: +44-20-7317-9120

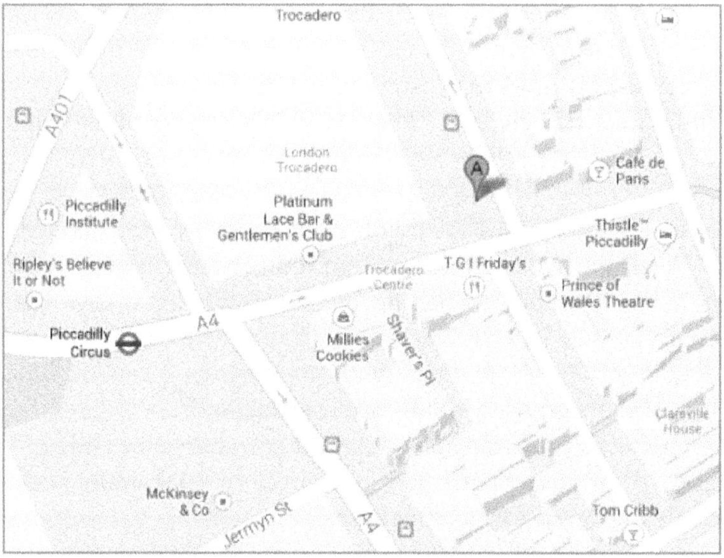

GoogleMap: http://goo.gl/maps/ev9YD

Supposedly the only place in London that started to offer this exquisite drink in 2011 priced at GBP70 (USD 116). Compared to the other coffee being served at this restaurant & nightclub at GBP 4 (USD 7), the current price for a cup of Kopi Luwak is GBP 30 (USD 50). Around 7grams of coffee is brewed and served in a heated designer cup with or without sugar. The coffee is much less acidic, has a frothy top layer, thick consistency, intense aroma and is delightfully smooth with a delicate aftertaste of a caramel.

2. Urban Coffee Company, Birmingham, UK

Website: http://www.urbancoffee.co.uk/2011/03/kopi-luwak/

Address:
30 Church Street,
Colmore Business District, Birmingham, B3 2NP, UK

Phone: +44-121-236-0207

GoogleMap: http://goo.gl/maps/9T01N

Located in Birmingham, Urban Coffee Company is the other place in UK that offers all coffee connoisseurs the Kop Luwak experience. Whether you want a ready-to-drink beverage or want to take home Kopi Luwak ground or beans, this is one place in the UK where you will find quality. If you live in Birmingham, or just visiting, visit Urban Coffee Company and try the world's best and most expensive coffee.

Chapter 6: Around the World for Kopi Luwak

USA

1. Funnel Mill, Santa Monica, California

Website: http://www.funnelmill.com/

Address:
Funnel Mill of Santa Monica
930 Broadway, Ste A, Santa Monica, CA 90401, USA

Phone: +1-310-393-1617

Google Map: http://goo.gl/maps/JZlwP

The first name in the list! This is one place to try out the best, most expensive and highest quality coffees in the United States. These people excel when it comes to maintaining the quality of their coffees and there are excellent reviews from people who have tried Kopi Luwak from this coffee outlet. If Santa Monica is where you live, you are blessed with a coffee café like no other.

2. Georgio's Coffee Roasters, New York

Website: http://www.georgioscoffee.com/

Address:
Georgio's Coffee Roasters
1965 New Highway, Farmingdale, NY 1173, USA

Phone: +1-516-238-2999

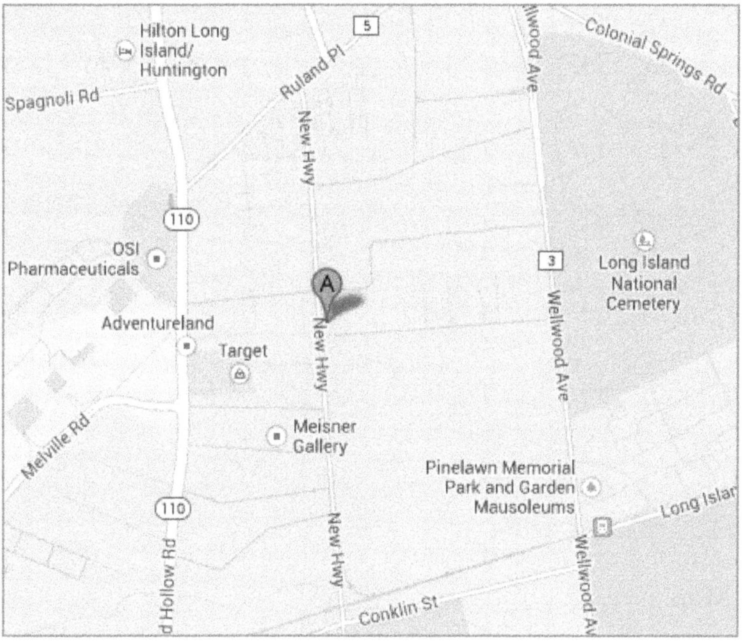

Google Map: http://goo.gl/maps/N7sJF

Again, known for their wide range of coffees from around the world, Georgio's Coffee Roasters is a famous name among coffee connoisseurs in New York. There are reviews where people claim they had an excellent time enjoying Kopi Luwak at the Georgio's Coffee Roasters. This is one place where you will definitely find the authentic taste and aroma of the real Kopi Luwak.

3. Barista Society Coffee Boutique, California

Website: http://www.baristasociety.com/

Address:
633 West 5th Street #250,
Los Angeles, CA 90071, USA

Phone: +1-213-444-3389

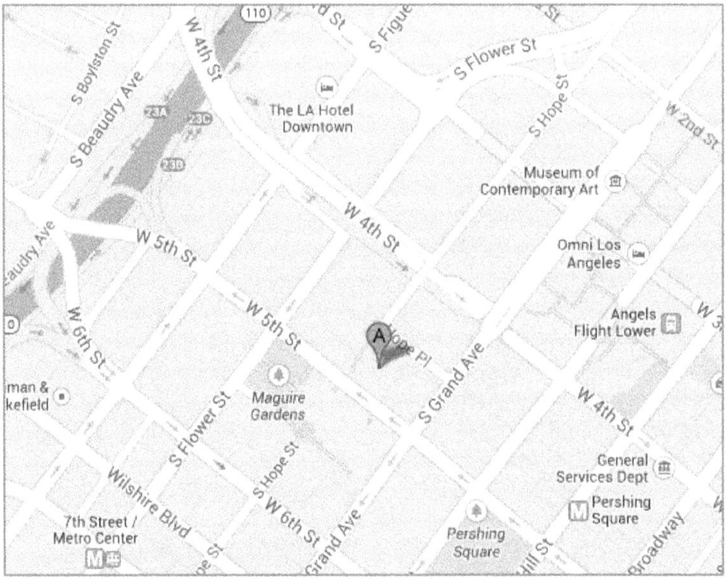

Google Map: http://goo.gl/maps/gW6bA

Looking for authentic Kopi Luwak coffee in California? Barista Society Coffee Boutique is the place to visit. Charging more than 90 US dollars (GBP 55) for a cup, these people promise to prepare your special cup of Kopi Luwak with real civet coffee beans. To make the most out of every penny spent on an expensive cup of coffee, visit Barista Society Coffee Boutique for a unique experience.

Indonesia

1. Seniman Coffee Studio, Ubud

Website: http://senimancoffee.com/

Address:
Jalan sriwedari, Ubud
Bali 80561, Indonesia

Phone: +62-361-972085

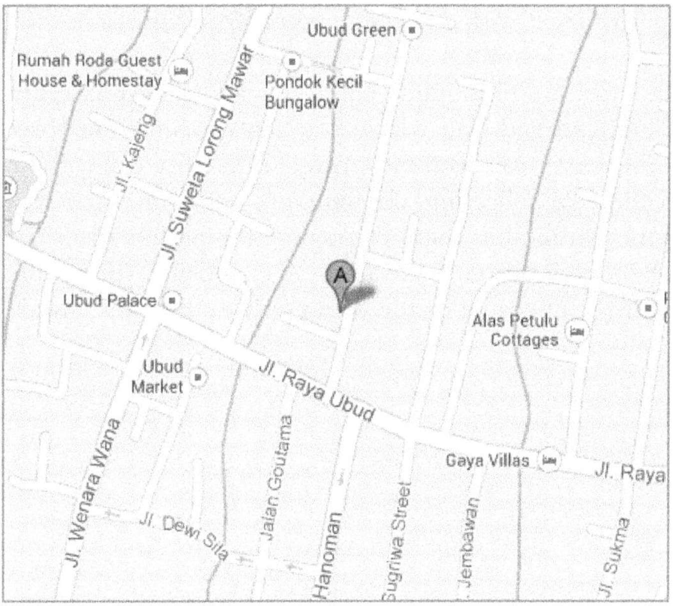

Google Map: http://goo.gl/maps/Np171

This is the place where you can find 100 percent Kopi Luwak without a doubt. Most coffee cafes in various islands of Indonesia are now offering Kopi Luwak, especially in Ubud, Sumatra and Bali. The best part about enjoying your Kopi Luwak at Seniman Coffee Studio is that most of it is processed and roasted before your eyes on site. What more could you ask for?

2. La Maison, Jakarta, Indonesia

One of the best coffee cafes in Jakarta, La Maison offers you a luxurious coffee drinking experience. With Kopi Luwak on the menu, you can have a lifetime experience at this place, enjoying the world's most expensive and exotic coffee with your friends and family.

The interior decors and the ambience of La Maison add to your overall experience. The coffee is served in beautiful coffee mugs to enhance your Kopi Luwak cup of coffee. If you are in Jakarta, don't forget to pamper yourself with an exotic cup of Kopi Luwak.

Note: Not only cafés and restaurants, there are various local farms in the islands of Sumatra and Bali where you can try authentic Kopi Luwak coffee. The best part about these places is that you can witness the entire procedure of collecting, cleaning, processing and roasting the coffee before you request them to prepare the perfect brew for you. This can be a very pleasant and exciting experience for people coming from a different corner of the world only to try Kopi Luwak.

3. Kopi Bali House, Bali

Website: http://www.bali-indonesia.com/magazine/kopi-bali-house.htm

Address:
Pertokoan Graha Niaga Sanur No 4,
Jl. Bypass Ngurah Rai 405E, Sanur, Indonesia

Phone: +62-361-270-990

Google Map: http://goo.gl/maps/nBmDZ

Opened in 2003, this place is famous for its good selection of coffees and food. The staff members hold a good knowledge on the variety of selection and you will find them well trained and professional.

The Gourmet coffee selection includes the raspberrian and avocado coffee along with the normal espressos and mochachinos, that will go hand in hand with a delicious selection of satay sticks, prawn crackers, and the traditional tipat cantok.

This place is much more than a Barista offering you coffee, that has an interior with stylish settings and artworks by Rudy Sri Handoko, Indonesian coffee painter. You can easily prepare and serve your Kopi Luwak coffee at the mini bar.

Australia

Hervey's Ranges Heritage Tea Rooms

Website: http://www.heritagetearooms.com.au/

Address:
Lot 6 Thorton's Gap Rd,
Hervey Range QLD 4817, Australia

Phone: +61-74778-0199

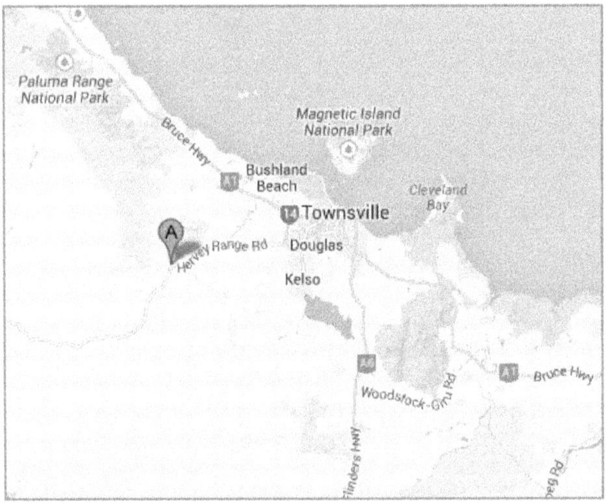

Google Map: http://goo.gl/maps/fIsxq

Get yourself pampered at the Hervey's Ranges Heritage Tea Rooms by grabbing a bag of Kopi Luwak coffee that you can prepare at home and share with friends and family. This is the only known place in Australia that claims to offer the most authentic Kopi Luwak coffee beans. If you are a true fan of Kopi Luwak, spend some money and grab a bag of Kopi Luwak. Worth trying!

Chapter 7: Interesting Facts on Kopi Luwak

These interesting facts on Kopi Luwak will give you some great information about this unique, exotic coffee as well as will refresh the overall concept of Kopi Luwak in your mind.

1. There are two distinct natural processes defined by Kopi Luwak: Farm and Wild. While many prefer wild Kopi Luwak, the idea is becoming extinct because all the civets are acquired by farms, where they are fed the best of beans and are provided the best atmosphere to excrete the highest quality Kopi Luwak beans.

2. Kopi Luwak can lose its original flavor and aroma and can taste like an ordinary coffee if over or under roasted. Recommended roasting for Kopi Luwak is neither too high nor too low. In order to keep the originality of this unique coffee, you need to roast it just right. The more you roast, the bolder and more intense it would taste, eliminating the variant originality of the coffee.

3. You can adjust the flavors of Kopi Luwak to make it a coffee that suits your preferences. With that said, yes you can add cream to your coffee and experience your very own Kopi Luwak.

4. As compared to Robusta, there is more variance in the acidity and taste of Arabica type Kopi Luwak coffee. Arabica Kopi Luwak is also regarded as much stronger in taste. On the other hand, Robusta is milder. In the western world, Arabica Kopi Luwak is significantly preferred over Robusta.

5. Although Kopi Luwak coffee is extracted from the excrement of the civet, the bacterial content is way lower than other coffees. This is due to the fermentation process that eliminates bacterium and protein, which change the taste and aroma and makes it more awesome.

6. The popularity and hype of Kopi Luwak as the world's most expensive coffee has hit the world. People in South Korea consider Kopi Luwak as a luxurious, prestige coffee with USD 90 (55 GBP) per cup.

7. In addition to using professional French press and class drip coffee equipment to make the perfect brew, you can simply boil Kopi Luwak coffee and enjoy a great experience.

8. Kopi Luwak coffee, which is excreted by the civet is considered safe for people suffering from ulcers.

Beware of the Imitation

Civet coffee imitation is basically an attempt to copy the aroma and unique taste of exotic Kopi Luwak coffee. The idea came into being as a response to civets becoming an endangered species. There was a decrease in the population of Asian palm civets, due to over hunting and loss of habitat.

The production of Kopi Luwak requires a great deal of workers, whether wild-gathered or farmed. The scarce productivity and the labour intensive work involved in the production contribute to the high cost of the coffee.

The outrageous price of Kopi Luwak coffee is another factor that persuades the search for introducing a new way to produce more and more Kopi Luwak and at a lower cost.

A study was conducted at the University of Guelph where the process of fermentation was examined. During the observation, the main focus was to learn about the stomach enzymes and acids of the animal that digests the beans and ferment them.

On the other hand, in the University of Florida, they revealed new ways to recreate how Kopi Luwak can be created without involving any animal or without allowing the coffee beans to pass through the digestive tract of any animal.

Later on, this technology was licensed to a Gainesville firm in Florida, Coffee Primero that now produces and offers that product at a competitive price, just like any other ordinary quality coffee.

The Chemistry behind the coffee

Research conducted by Massimo Marcone, a food scientist, at the University of Guelph, revealed that the endogenous digestive secretions of the civet seep into the coffee beans when they consume them. Proteolytic enzymes are carried by these secretions, which is responsible for breaking down the proteins of the beans, yielding more free amino acids and shorter peptides.

Since the protein is the driving factor behind the unique flavor of Kopi Luwak, there's a hypothesis that shifts the kinds and numbers of proteins present in beans after they are consumed by Asian palm civets to give them their unique taste.

Later, proteins also experience browning reactions in non-enzymatic Maillard brought about later by the roasting process. Also, the beans inside a civet begin to germinate due to malting, which controls the bitterness of the coffee.

On the outside, Massimo Marcone was not really sure about the safety of Kopi Luwak from his research. However, he later discovered that once the coffee beans are thoroughly washed, the level of harmful organisms become insignificant. Also, since coffee beans are roasted at high temperature, it has been cited that Kopi Luwak is safe for consumption.

In fact, some studies also support that Kopi Luwak is safe for ulcer patients. Due to the natural fermentation process, people who are allergic to coffee are said to easily digest Kopi Luwak. However, this is very subjective and should not be tried.

Best Reviewed Websites to Get Authentic Kopi Luwak at Your Doorstep

While many people prefer the experts to prepare a cup of coffee for them, especially when they are paying as high as USD 90 per cup (55 GBP), some like it to be a more personalized experience by preparing their cup of coffee themselves.

Also, there are some coffee enthusiasts who will go around the world to get their hands on the best, authentic and most expensive coffee in the world. Others prefer to surf the Internet and order a bag of happiness from the most reliable sources right to their doorstep for convenience's sake.

If you are the latter one, the information shared here will definitely help you. As you all know, Kopi Luwak is an extremely scarce commodity. It is not possible to open an outlet or make Kopi Luwak available in all countries and all cities. Sometimes, you are required to drive a few kilometres or miles to buy the perfect Kopi Luwak beans. However, with advancement in technology and more and more people inclined towards comfort shopping through the internet, people hardly step out in a challenging hunt like this one.

They believe it is better to stay within the comfort of their homes and order Kopi Luwak from the most reliable sources available online. Here I have shared some top sites that offer their Kopi Luwak delivery service around the world. Check out the listed websites below and see which one delivers to your destination and at what price.

1. Origano Luwak Coffee
http://www.origanoluwakcoffee.com/index.php?route=common/home

2. Real Kopi Luwak
http://www.realkopiluwak.com/

3. Kopi Luwak Online
http://kopiluwakonline.com/index.html

4. Luwak Café
http://www.luwakcafe.com/

5. Kopi Luwak Direct
http://kopiluwakdirect.com/

6. Luwak Coffee
http://www.animalcoffee.com/

These online websites offer free shipping to various countries and cities. If this is your cup of coffee, try one now and experience drinking the best coffee available in the world.

Conclusion: Get the Best Coffee for That Top Dollar

You are spending money; a lot of it! Do not compromise with the quality you get. For that top dollar, get your hands on the best and most authentic Kopi Luwak coffee in the world. Currently selling for more than USD 90 per cup (55 GBP) and USD 400 to USD 600 per pound (GBP 235 to GBP 355), the coffee is the rarest and most unique when it comes to flavor and aroma.

Drinking a coffee that is not only expensive but rare is indeed a privilege. Make the most out of this luxury coffee drinking experience and enjoy every drop of it by implementing the information available in the book. I have tried and covered every possible detail about Kopi Luwak in this book so that you became familiar with Kopi Luwak before trying it out. If the idea of civet poop coffee seems strange and interesting to you at the same time and if you really want to give this one a shot, the time is now.

Don't wait until the coffee disappears again. Regardless of which part in the world you are, Kopi Luwak will find its way to you if you want it. Order it online or travel all the way to Indonesia to have a real life experience; Kopi Luwak is a beverage worth trying.

With all the information available in this book, the right time to give the sizzling cup of coffee a try is now. So research more and do some more homework if you like and order from the most authentic retailers and online stores.

Enjoy every sip of it like you will never get it again.
Good luck!

FAQ

1. **Why Robusta Kopi Luwak and Arabica Kopi Luwak taste different?**

It's important to find out from which area Kopi Luwak is coming from. Luwaks in the wild eat the ripest coffee berries from the plantation they can access within their habitat. So this produces Arabica and Robusta Kopi Luwak.

However, the best quality Kopi Luwak will be the one that is collected from the good quality Arabica coffee plantation. For instance, it is believed that the Kopi Luwak from Sumatra is different from Kopi Luwaks in Bali because the Arabica beans coffee from where they are produced also differ in taste.

2. **How long will my Kopi Luwak stay fresh?**

The most important thing to keep in mind is that Luwak coffee is not wine. Its taste will not improve as it ages. Also, always remember that whole coffee beans stay fresh for longer, precisely up to 4 to 6 weeks as compared to ground coffee. However, it is highly recommended to enjoy it sooner to get a better, fresher taste.

Kopi Luwak is more permeable as compared to regular coffee. This is due to the positive effect of the natural enzymes in the digestive system of a civet. The fabulous taste and aroma are more fleeting in contrast with other types of coffees.

3. What is the best way to store Kopi Luwak?

All coffees, including Kopi Luwak, should never be stored in a refrigerator. As far as storing in the freezer is concerned, that is explained in detail in the book. However, storing coffee is risky, especially when it comes to Kopi Luwak.

Beans that cost you a fortune cannot be wasted. You should choose the best storage method to ensure the freshness and originality of the rarest coffee beans in the world lasts as long as possible. Although, it is highly recommended to consume the coffee sooner to experience the original and unique flavors and taste of the coffee, but in case you need to store it, always use a container or storage place that is free from light, air, moisture and heat.

4. Can you prepare Kopi Luwak with cream and sweeteners?

One thing should not change; you should always drink coffee the way you like it. It is possible to make your Kopi Luwak experience personalized, especially if you are preparing coffee at home. Adjust the flavors by adding creamers or sweeteners as you like. However, experts suggest that you should at least try the original brewed Kopi Luwak once before making any additions to experience what a luxury, exotic coffee that is the most expensive coffee in the world, tastes like.

Relevant Sources

Source of Content:

http://blog.origanoluwakcoffee.com/10-facts-about-kopi-luwak-you-should-know

http://www.amazon.com/Dont-Kopi-Luwak-Coffee-Before-ebook/dp/B0075W1MFI

http://www.realkopiluwak.com/intro-real-kopi-luwak/

http://coffeetea.about.com/library/glossary/bldef_kopiluwak.htm

http://kopi-luwak.com/about-us/

http://coffeetea.about.com/cs/kindsofcoffee/a/aakopiluwak.htm

http://coffeetea.about.com/od/coffeerecipes/

http://www.kopiluwakonline.com/

http://kopiluwakonline.com/howtomapelaa.html

http://www.volcanicacoffee.com/estate-coffee/kopi-luwak-coffee.htm

http://www.luwakcafe.com/about/

http://www.theloveofcoffee.co.uk/kopi-luwak-civet-cat-coffee-543-p.asp

http://www.realkopiluwak.com/perfect-cup/

http://www.realkopiluwak.com/about-luwak/

http://www.realkopiluwak.com/warning/

Relevant Sources

http://www.wspa.org.uk/latestnews/2013/Harrods_takes_Kopi_Luwak_off_sale.aspx

http://luwakkopi.com/773.html

http://www.coffeestrategies.com/2011/12/07/kopi-luwak-curiosity-kills-civet-cats

http://www.scaa.org/chronicle/2011/11/02/the-value-of-a-good-story-or-how-to-turn-poop-into-gold/

http://coffeeproject.com/shop/magento/beans

For more information, please go to the following site:
http://www.kopiluwakcoffeefacts.com/

Relevant Sources

Source of Images:

http://upload.wikimedia.org/wikipedia/commons/f/fa/Kopi_Luwak-01.jpg

http://upload.wikimedia.org/wikipedia/commons/f/f7/Luwak.jpg

http://upload.wikimedia.org/wikipedia/commons/c/ce/Asian_Palm_Civet_Over_A_Tree.jpg

http://upload.wikimedia.org/wikipedia/commons/2/28/Luwak-Katze_in_Kepahiang.jpg

http://farm4.staticflickr.com/3147/2620250456_7dc5107323_o.jpg

http://upload.wikimedia.org/wikipedia/commons/thumb/8/89/Moka_Pezzetti_per_alimenti_08.jpg/768px-Moka_Pezzetti_per_alimenti_08.jpg

http://upload.wikimedia.org/wikipedia/commons/9/92/Manual_coffee_preperation.jpg

Index

Index

Lightning Source UK Ltd.
Milton Keynes UK
UKHW021312100820
367992UK00011B/2387

9 780992 798710